TROPICAL LYNX'S LOVER

ZOE CHANT

SHIFTING SANDS RESORT

This book is part of a complete series, with recurring characters, but it does stand alone, with a satisfying happy-ever-after and no cliffhangers. Escape to Shifting Sands Resort and buckle up for a ten-book binge-read that will take you on a wild ride with a thrilling conclusion!

See also: the Shifting Sands Resort Omnibus, 4 volumes that include all the books, short stories, novellas, and three exclusive stories, all in the author's preferred reading order, available in ebook, paperback, audiobook, and hardcover!

---

*T*ravis James stumbled into the empty staff house, dropping his toolbox just inside the door, where he also took off his sodden shoes and shrugged the work gloves off his hands to flop onto the floor like small dead things.

His lynx stirred at the idea of small dead things, twitching metaphorical ears in interest, then expressing disdain. *Living things are more fun to chase,* Lynx told him.

That eliminates us as "fun," Travis told him in return.

He felt like a zombie, limbs numb with exhaustion. Only shifter strength kept him stumbling forward at this point, and only hunger made him stagger into the kitchen instead of immediately finding his bed.

The harvest gold fridge revealed a treasure trove of food: cold cuts, fruit, deviled eggs, cold grilled fish, and even a few legs of crab standing guard over the bottom shelf, all of it leftover from the resort buffet. A cling-wrapped slice of cake said "Breck's. Eat at your own risk." Someone had left a sticky note on it in different handwriting: "I licked it."

"Don't eat Breck's cake," a voice behind him startled him, and only Travis' shifter-quick reflexes kept him from banging his head into the refrigerator door.

Bastian was standing at the door to the kitchen, and it took Travis a moment to realize that he looked strange because he was wearing something other than his bright-colored lifeguard uniform. The resort polo shirt was unexpected over the dragon shifter's chest, and the khaki pants made Travis realize he'd never seen Bastian out of shorts.

"At this point, spit doesn't scare me," Travis told him with a tired grin.

"You look like hell," Bastian told him frankly.

"Feel like it, too," Travis said briefly. "Been a long couple of weeks."

That was an understatement.

It had been an insane, demanding several weeks, as Shifting Sands Resort hosted the World Mr. Shifter male pageant.

Booked to capacity, as Travis suspected it had never been, the resort had performed well for a facility built in the eighties. Even though Scarlet had modernized most of it over the past several years following its long period of abandonment, it had required a flurry of last minute upgrades and Travis had spent the weeks leading up to the event putting cottages back into service, checking and monitoring the aging septic system, and upgrading the wiring and water heaters in anticipation of the influx of guests.

Considering how many people had descended on the resort, it had all gone very smoothly, Travis thought.

But that didn't mean it hadn't been a lot of very long days, running from task to task. The air conditioner in the hotel was down as much as it was up, and there wasn't a day that there wasn't some minor plumbing emergency.

The laundry load had been higher than anyone had anticipated, and though Breck was able to help with some of the
mechanical work, and most of the staff knew how to
respond to blown fuses, Travis had been required to do any
of the finesse work on the wiring, and troubleshoot the
inevitable problems you had with generators run at full
capacity for so long. Only he could do work that required
welding or pipe replacement.

"You should get some sleep," Bastian advised.

"Oh, I plan to," Travis said. "Scarlet told me that if I
showed my face before noon, she'd fire me. I'm pretty sure
she wasn't kidding." The red-haired owner of the resort
was not one to be trifled with.

"You'll miss a helluva party," Bastian laughed. "And
I've got to get down to it now. Tex isn't back, so I've got to
run the beach bar."

"Better you than me," Travis told him.

"You going to need any help?" Bastian asked,
concerned.

Travis realized that he'd been staring blankly, standing
with the fridge open and the cold air swirling over his feet.
He shook his head. "Nah, I got it. Just going to have some
food and then sleep until noon, as commanded."

"You do that," Bastian agreed, and he disappeared
from the doorway. The front door slammed, and Travis
could hear footsteps crunching away in the gravel through
the open windows.

Travis left the cake alone, and went for a pile of meat.
A slice of bread from the sealed loaf bin on the counter
folded around it to complete the sandwich; he didn't
bother with condiments or a plate. By the time he made it
back to his bedroom, it was gone, all the crumbs inhaled,
and he felt full enough to sleep.

He shucked off the filthy staff polo shirt, making his

shoulders ache in new ways, and unbuttoned his heavy canvas pants.

The bed had been made up, though Travis was sure he had left it in disarray after too few hours of sleep far too many hours before. He was touched. The staff was usually self-sufficient about their own housekeeping, so one of his co-workers must have done it for him as a personal favor. The sheets even smelled clean, and Travis sighed. There was no way he was going to put his filthy body in those linens.

Not bothering with a bathrobe, Travis slipped his briefs off to join the grime-stiff pants and walked naked back out into the hall to the shared bathroom.

The marble and tile room that greeted him was more like a Greek steamhouse than a mere staff bathroom, even at an upscale resort like Shifting Sands Resort. It had not only a shower and separate tub, but also a steam room and a completely private water closet. The vanity had three separate sinks below an expanse of framed mirror.

Travis caught a glimpse of himself and grimaced.

He looked like a zombie as well as feeling like one. Fast-healing bruises from crawling under the cottages fixing plumbing problems showed purple through his golden skin along one flank. There was a scratch along one arm from a stray wire while fixing the circuitry for the ailing air conditioner in the hotel. The circles beneath his eyes were distinctly unflattering, and his short dark hair was stiff and wild with sweat and grease.

He turned away, and pulled the shower control to full heat and full strength, standing in the stream even before the heat from the tank had reached the shower. The rest of the staff would be away for hours; the World Mr. Shifter event was in its final, glorious throes, and the wrap-up party on the beach would keep the rest of the staff busy until morning. Travis didn't have to worry about saving any of the precious hot water for anyone else.

The water was running scalding hot now, and Travis lay his brow against the steamy tile and let it beat the stiffness out of his tired muscles.

There was a tremendous amount of satisfaction from the work. He took pride in keeping Shifting Sands running smoothly, and the staff was more like family than simply co-workers. The perks of the job included a beautiful place to live, all of the gourmet food he could eat, and most of the time, the workload was minimal. Scarlet listened to his advice when it came to remodeling and buying new equipment, and was fair and clear in her expectations.

It wasn't the work that was leaving Travis feeling hollow. He loved Shifting Sands, from the persnickety power grid to the steep, sprawling gravel paths. The resort was home, in a bone-deep way that even his Native village in Alaska had never been, and he was proud of how beautiful and functional it was, and how much it had improved in the past few years.

Maybe it was just exhaustion, making him feel like like something was missing.

Travis leaned against the shower control to turn it off, and stood there a weary moment, dripping.

The empty house felt unexpectedly lonely.

It took a ridiculous amount of time to reach for a towel and give himself a cursory pat-down. Scarlet didn't skimp on towels, so the thick, fluffy terrycloth absorbed most of the water even with halfhearted application. Travis barely got it back onto his towel hook before staggering back to his bedroom.

Even the fireworks couldn't keep him awake after that.

2

---

*J*ennavivianna Smith wasn't floating.

For the first time in a very long time, she wasn't floating.

She wasn't all-Jenny, yet, but she wasn't as not-Jenny as she had been, and she kept her eyes screwed shut for a while after she was actually awake, trying to process what had happened.

"You're not sleeping anymore!"

At first, Jenny thought that it was her own thoughts. Her own, weirdly divided thoughts. The otter inside her that wasn't her, but was, all at once.

"You can't fool me," the voice said firmly, and Jenny remembered.

She remembered Gizelle, the slight, salt-and-pepper-haired woman who had talked her back into human form, and remembered seeing Fred again and feeling the sting of his betrayal, and Laura, oh, Laura! Her twin was there in her head again, that unspoken connection they'd always had was back and as strong and comforting as it had always been, even when they were at odds, or miles apart.

She opened her eyes. She was in a little square of neat lawn near a white gravel path, tall, flowering jungle brush on all sides. She could hear the ocean, and smell its sharp, salty tang, but she couldn't see anything through the dense foliage.

Gizelle was kneeling above her, hair wild around her face, big eyes earnest. "Come on, then, you've had a good sleep."

Jenny opened her mouth to protest that the sleep had been restless, and full of floating dreams, but it came out as half-trill and half-purr, and she snapped otter jaws together again.

"It takes a little while, that's all. Come and walk on two legs with me. See your sister!"

Jenny balked. The last time she had changed from otter to human, it had burned. She remembered the feeling of her bones cracking and resetting, the muscles stretching impossibly, the tendons snapping into new places.

"Don't be afraid," Gizelle said coaxingly.

"Don't baby me," Jenny wanted to tell her, but couldn't, through otter teeth. Nothing frustrated her more than being patronized.

Don't act like a baby, then, her otter told her. Its voice in her head was not scornful, exactly, but teasing, prodding.

Jenny felt more stung than she knew she ought to. *I'm not being a baby.*

Of course you aren't, her otter mocked. *You're a 'grown-up' coward.*

With an otter sigh of frustration, Jenny stretched.

At first, it was simply a stretch of otter limbs, then Jenny focused furiously, remembering human arms and human legs, and she reached and wrenched herself back into her own form.

Gizelle clapped her hands in delight as Jenny lay on the

ground, naked and panting. "Good job!" she said enthusiastically.

"Don't baby me," Jenny was finally able to say, breathlessly.

Then don't-

Shut up. Jenny was dismayed to see that her fingers were still slightly webbed, and tipped with sharp claws. She ran her tongue over teeth that were too sharp and grimaced.

Gizelle took no notice of Jenny's crabbiness, simply offering her hands to stand up.

Let's go run around on those human legs you love so much, her otter suggested. *Maybe go swimming at the beach.*

I'm a little naked, Jenny reminded her, accepting Gizelle's offered hands and climbing to her feet.

I know, her otter purred back at her, full of mischief. Images of admiring men accompanied the rejoinder. Jenny felt her skin heat, hating herself for how the idea stirred in her loins.

"How do you do this?" Jenny demanded of Gizelle, standing unsteadily.

"I know, it's weird there's only two of them," Gizelle said comfortingly.

"Only two?" Jenny asked. Were there shifters with more than one extra voice?

"You just have to shift your weight between each one, and not think about it too much to keep your balance."

When Jenny looked blankly at her, Gizelle scampered away and ran in a circle. "Like this!" she called merrily.

"You meant *legs*," Jenny realized. "Only two *legs*."

Returning, Gizelle said, "Of course I meant *legs*. What else would I mean?"

"I thought you meant voices," Jenny said, feeling foolish.

"There are *always* more than two voices," Gizelle said

solemnly, eyes big in her face.

Jenny had just started feeling like things made sense, and then suddenly she didn't again. She could feel her otter's amusement, and shunted it away. "There's more?" she said unhappily. She could barely stand otter's demanding voice, should she expect more of them?

"Voices that whisper. Voices in the sky with no sun. Feathered voices. Voices that-"

"Gizelle," said a new voice, gently chiding.

Jenny turned, half-crouching, and nearly let her otter take control of her skin again instinctively. *No!* she thought fiercely, fighting to stay in human skin.

The red-haired woman from the night before stood at the opening in the hedge by the white path. She was neatly dressed, and Jenny was relieved to see that she was holding clothing in her hand.

It was her own dress, Jenny realized, and more memories flooded back. Laura, her twin, had come to the resort pretending to be Jenny, and of course she would have packed Jenny's clothing for the trip.

Naked would be more fun, her otter pouted at her.

Jenny ignored the voice.

"I'm Scarlet," the woman said, handing her the dress and looking politely aside while Jenny struggled to put it on. "I run Shifting Sands."

Jenny, still trying to work out how to get her head through the neckhole and feeling stumped by the armholes, was keenly aware of Gizelle staring at her.

"Gizelle," Scarlet said kindly.

"She's really bad at that," Gizelle said frankly.

"I need you to help Graham in the upper gardens, please." Scarlet's tone made it sound less like a request and more like a royal command.

Triumphant at last over the openings in the dress,

Jenny pulled it fiercely down over her generous curves.

"Bye!" said Gizelle merrily, and she skipped off across the lawn and out the way Scarlet had come. Her footsteps were quiet on the gravel, and Jenny realized she was barefoot.

"I apologize for Gizelle," Scarlet said, sounding not the slightest bit apologetic. "She has taken great interest in you."

"She's not neurotypical, is she," Jenny observed. It felt ironic to say so, since she felt so much less than normal herself.

Normal is boring, her otter told her.

"We released Gizelle from a madman's prison less than a year ago and it took her a long time to shift from her gazelle form," Scarlet explained. "She remembers nothing about her life in his zoo. We have no idea how old she is, or where she came from before then. She may even have been born there." She gave Jenny an intense, appraising look. "How much do *you* remember?"

Jenny gazed back at Scarlet without seeing her. "I remember driving. It was Laura's car, I was just going to get her a few things from the supermarket. There was an explosion — I lost control of the car, and it went off a curve. I remember going through the guardrail..."

She shuddered, remembering the scream of metal and the drop into the shattering ocean below, hitting her head, waves and water and sinking...

Comfort came from an unexpected source.

I caught you. I was there for you.

Jenny pushed back. She didn't want to be grateful to the interloper in her head.

"I shifted," she said woodenly. "I've never shifted before. I didn't know I could. I don't think I could, before."

Scarlet listened, but offered no comment.

Jenny worked her mouth, trying to find words for what came next. She had been more otter than herself, eating, swimming, floating in sleep. She was drawn south, swimming earnestly, day after day, through currents that became gradually warmer.

"I found Laura after her boat exploded. I didn't really think about things, only knew that I had to help her, and where I could find that help."

"Shifting Sands was always meant to be a safe haven for shifters," Scarlet said, nodding.

Jenny felt her eyebrows scrunch together. "Shifting… Sands. I worked on the contract for this place." Life before this seemed impossibly distant and long ago. "I was — I am — a lawyer."

"What else do you remember?" Scarlet asked gently.

"I remember Fred," Jenny said firmly. "He betrayed us. He was the one who sabotaged Laura's car, and her boat. And… our parents. He killed our parents, so long ago." Somehow, it stung as much now as it had when Jenny had first uncovered the treachery, weeks ago.

"He's in custody," Scarlet promised fiercely. "He will never be able to hurt you again."

Jenny tried to take comfort in the idea, and nodded.

Somewhere, far away, there was a beep of a car horn and shouting voices, and Scarlet frowned. "Let me take you to the dining hall. You've missed lunch, but there's a buffet available and you must be hungry after your long ordeal."

On cue, Jenny's stomach rumbled, and she and her otter finally agreed on something.

"I'm famished," she admitted. Then she added, "Just please, tell me I don't have to eat raw fish or urchins for a long, long time."

She didn't think she would ever enjoy a sushi bar again.

$\mathcal{T}$ravis rolled out bed when he woke up, habit driving him to get dressed before he registered that it was already midday, and that he actually felt well-rested.

He got dressed and wandered to the kitchen to appease Lynx's cries for food, and found a quarter of a pie dish full of shrimp kale quiche with his name on it. The cake had a new note on it: "Dragon germs don't scare me."

Through the open windows of the house, he could hear distant sounds of the resort below, the ocean and the pool waterfalls making a pleasant backdrop to the hum of activity. It was quieter than the day before. Travis imagined the last guests, nursing hangovers, hauling their luggage to turn in their keys and file into the van that would take them to the little airfield on the far side of the island. The resort staff would spend the day cleaning up at a leisurely pace, putting everything back in order for the next, much smaller, wave of guests.

Quiche inhaled, Travis went to find his tools. He knew there would be work for him today, but he also knew that the insane pressure of the last few weeks was lifted, and his steps felt light and eager for the first time in a long time. His work gloves and boots had been dried, shaken out, and hung up. Travis gave a crooked smile for the thoughtfulness of his housemates.

His feet automatically took him to the largest building on the resort, the building that held the dining hall, kitchen, and conference room on the top level, the bar and mechanical rooms on the next level down, overlooking the pool below. The staff bulletin board in the conference room was where the calendar was posted, and where they left notes for each other about problems that needed fixed.

The calendar was marked "Travis: DAY OFF" and "Breck: Return the keys to rooms 7 and 12." The dry-erase board had a note: "Fix washer four." In new handwriting someone had added, "And dryer three."

Knowing he didn't have to handle it perversely made Travis want to.

There was singing coming from the kitchen, a tragic opera song in Chef's booming bass voice. Travis smiled to remember that Magnolia would be returning any day. The resort would feel normal again.

But normal still didn't feel... complete.

"Travis! What are you doing up so early?" How Breck, the head waiter, managed to look so fresh and energetic after what Travis knew could only have been a few hours of sleep was a mystery.

"It's after noon," Travis said skeptically.

"You still look like you need a week of sleep," the leopard shifter said critically.

"Thanks!"

"You're off the books today," Breck reminded him, frowning at the toolbox. "There are only about four guests left, so don't sweat anything."

"There will be more coming, though," Travis reminded him.

Breck was looking at the calendar and checking the notes. "Not until tomorrow, and next week will be cake compared to the last few." He gave Travis a suspicious look. "Speaking of…"

"I didn't touch your cake."

Breck gave him a theatrically skeptical look, then took off towards the kitchen, opening the door with a surprisingly good harmony to Chef's song.

Travis shook his head and walked past the kitchen door as it swung shut, heading for the back staff stairs down to the laundry and mechanical room.

The relative stillness of the pool deck and the bar was welcome; it was strange, after the past few days, not to have to elbow through throngs of guests to get anywhere. Tex was behind the bar, and his new mate sat before him on a bar stool.

Our *mate*, Lynx said, unexpectedly in his head, and Travis had to freeze at the intensity of it.

That's Tex's mate, Travis assured him, shaken. Yes, she was a gorgeous woman, and Tex was lucky to have her, with that velvety dark skin and those beautiful curves, but that he would even give her a second glance felt like betrayal.

No, Lynx growled. *She's ours.*

All Travis could do was stare.

*J*enny followed Scarlet up the winding white path to a pool deck that she vaguely remembered from the previous night. It looked quite different in daylight, brilliantly gleaming in the tropical sun. It was bigger than it had looked in the faint light of pre-dawn, and was edged with palm trees. What had only been the sound of splashing water proved to be twin waterfalls, flanking a grand staircase that came down into the pool from the upper deck.

Jenny was grateful for the dress Scarlet had brought her, but found herself keenly aware that she was wearing no underthings beneath it as Scarlet led her between scattered sun chairs. She was glad to see very few people, most of them looking hungover and dragging luggage.

"I suspect that Gizelle was not the best person to wake up to in a new place," Scarlet explained. "But she may be uniquely suited to helping you with your new shifting abilities, and she seems to want to. I apologize for not being able to stay longer and help you get situated, but I had a great deal of paperwork to do in the wake of your arrival."

It wasn't quite an accusation.

"I'm sorry, I don't know when I will be able to pay you for our stay," Jenny said hesitantly. "The money is going to be tied up in legal battles for a while." The life insurance money that had been denied to Jenny and Laura when her parents had been murdered would be difficult to access while the justice system unraveled the depths of Fred's activity. Jenny's head hurt, thinking about the layers of bureaucracy they were going to have to go through to put the whole sordid affair to rest. She usually loved a messy challenge to unravel; that was part of the reason she had dived into a career in law. But right now, the idea of facing anything more complicated than a sandwich felt over-whelming. She wasn't even sure if she'd be able to access her own slim accounts; her laptop had been destroyed and she couldn't remember any of the details or login credentials.

Scarlet looked as if she had been deeply offended. "You are our guest," she said in icy tones. "I will put you in touch with some legal council I have connections with once you feel up to it." Her skeptical tone made Jenny suspect Scarlet rather doubted her ability whether she felt 'up to it' or not.

The red-haired woman led her up a wide flight of stairs up to a deck that overlooked the pool and a collection of chairs and tables outside of an open bar. Tinny country music in Spanish was playing on a radio and Jenny's chest squeezed at the familiar sight of her wolf shifter sister, sitting in front of the bar.

"Jenny!" Laura leaped up from the barstool and tackled Jenny in a fierce hug.

Jenny was not sure if she should weep on Laura's shoulder or flee, suddenly feeling terribly unsteady. She clung to Laura much longer than she normally would have, and awkwardly hid her webbed hands behind her when they finally ended the embrace.

"Jenny," Laura said nervously. "I want you to meet Tex. Or, er, meet him again."

Tex was leaning over the bar, and Jenny immediately remembered his bear smell, and the beat up cowboy hat he was wearing from the night before. "I'm sorry about the hat," she said hesitantly.

There was something else familiar about him, and she couldn't put her finger on it until Tex's handsome face split into a grin and he put fingers automatically to the rim of the hat in question. "You don't have anything to apologize for, ma'am," he drawled, and he extended his hand to shake.

Jenny stared. "You're the bartender! From Texas!" It had been at least five years ago that they'd met; he'd been an absolute gentleman, and she'd been an embarrassment.

Tex smiled at her. "I am indeed the bartender from Texas."

Jenny winced to hear how stupid it sounded. His name was Tex, and he was standing behind the bar. "The other bar, I mean the bar *in* Texas." She realized Tex still had his hand out, but it had been offered too long now, and she didn't want to put her webbed fingers in his.

Laura sidled up beside her as Tex casually took his hand back, and Jenny could feel the energy and excitement that beamed from her. "Jenny, Tex is my mate."

Jenny looked from one of them to the other, marveling at the way they gazed at each other. She had never seen Laura look so content.

She started to smile, genuinely glad that her twin had found happiness, then remembered her pointed teeth and stopped. "Congratulations," she said, strained.

Scarlet had been waiting through the introductions

impatiently, and finally said, so politely that it was verging on cold, "Please excuse me, I have a great deal to do." And she tapped off with a distinctive click from her low-heeled shoes over the tile.

"I've got the number from her for a guy back in America who works for a government shifter agency," Laura said, patting the barstool next to her. "He can expedite having Fred turned over to US custody, and help with getting the insurance money sorted. He may even be able to get things in motion regarding getting the cartel behind bars, I'll have to talk to him about that."

Jenny sat numbly on the stool and stared at her sister. Where had this capable, confident woman come from? How the tables had turned! Now, *she* felt like the screw-up sister, hardly able to make sense of simple words, and not even able to shift fully into her human form. She curled her webbed fingers into balls and winced when the claws scratched her palms.

I'm hungry, her otter insisted. Something smelled heavenly.

"There was food?" she said faintly. She didn't want otter to drag her out into the ocean after fresh fish for lack of options.

Laura and Tex both jumped. "Of course!" Laura said. "There's a buffet just upstairs, you sit here and I'll bring you a plate."

"I could get it," Tex offered, but Laura brushed him off.

"I know what she likes!"

They exchanged a swift kiss so intense that it made Jenny look away in embarrassment, and then Laura was slipping away through the backdoor of the bar, presumably to stairs that would take her up to the deck above them where the heavenly smells were coming from.

Tex put a bowl of mixed nuts in front of her, and poured a tall glass of pale juice. "You should get something in your stomach," he advised kindly.

Jenny tried to keep her hands low, positioning the glass between her fingers and Tex as best as she could. He seemed to sense her hesitation, and turned away to do obvious busywork at the far end of the bar. "I'm glad to see you up and about," he said without pressure. "Your sister is so happy to have you back again."

The drink proved to be lemonade, sweet and tangy, but not too strong. Jenny sipped it down eagerly and emptied the bowl of nuts without thinking about it.

Easing her hunger didn't bring the clarity of thought that Jenny had hoped for, but it did ease the overbearing intensity of her otter's presence a little.

She turned in her chair and looked out over the deck. Sunlight danced over the rippled surface of the pool, and dappled through the shade from the palm trees. The place had this strange sense of promise to it that Jenny had never felt before.

I'm hungry, her otter told her, and it wasn't the kind of hunger that a bowl of nuts was going to touch.

There was a man standing at one of the doors marked 'Staff Only' and Jenny tried not to stare. He was all lean strength, the staff polo shirt doing nothing to mask the muscles of his shoulders and arms. She thought he was Asian at first, with short, dark hair and golden skin, then he turned away from her abruptly, and the planes of his cheeks as the sun hit them made her think 'Native.'

He was gorgeous, like a sculpture, or a model, and Jenny was keenly reminded that she was still not wearing underwear. She squirmed on her stool, unable to look away as he yanked the door open and disappeared inside.

*I'm **hungry***, her otter repeated ferociously, and Jenny

shuddered and cringed at the intensity and immediacy of it. If the otter had her way, they'd be scurrying over the white tile to catch the man, and her otter had very specific ideas of what they'd be doing with him once they caught him, regardless of where they were or who else was there.

She was still fighting down the carnal wave of need and animal lust when Laura returned with a platter full of Jenny's favorite food: glistening cubes of fresh fruit and cottage cheese, and a heaping green salad with slices of eggs and avocado, scattered with squares of real bacon and feta cheese and drizzled with a vinaigrette. A roll so fresh it was still warm topped off the plate.

Jenny was achingly glad there wasn't a hint of fish or seafood on the plate, and with a whimper, she fell upon it, channeling all of her energy to eating.

$\mathcal{T}$ravis shut the door to the laundry room without flipping on the light switch and leaned against it in the dark, breathing as heavily as if he'd just run a marathon.

Lynx, in his head, was suggesting other courses of action. Filthy, detailed suggestions that made Travis keenly aware of how long it had been since any hand but his own had been in contact with certain parts.

That's Tex's mate, he insisted desperately. *She's gorgeous, but she's not ours.* He had to wonder why Lynx hadn't had this reaction the first few times they'd met, but why-ever that was, he wasn't going to betray his code of conduct and so much as sniff in her direction if she belonged to someone else.

Travis turned on the light switch and winced in the harsh light. He had to adjust himself to kneel at the service port for the washer in question. Several of the other washers were churning along in their duties, and the piles of dirty laundry were epic, even though housekeeping was probably still stripping down beds as guests checked out.

She has a service port we could use, Lynx said slyly.

You are a dirty, dirty tomcat who ought to be fixed, Travis replied. *Tex's mate, remember.* **Tex's mate!**

He replaced the worn-out motor bearing that he knew was the cause of the washer's problem, gritting his teeth and ignoring Lynx's continued insistence that they fling the door to the mechanical room open and chase their mate down, fighting off Tex or anyone else who tried to stand in their way.

The dryer fuse was next to replace, as Lynx continued to demand that they pursue her, now, now, now, and Travis tried to shut out his persistent voice. Travis even moved laundry from the washer to the dryer when one of them stopped, and loaded up the two empty machines with new laundry from the piles.

He might have hidden in the mechanical room until night, but Lydia, the black swan shifter who ran the spa, opened the door and wheeled in a cart of laundry.

"Don't you have the day off?" she asked, in her rich Spanish accent.

"I slept in," Travis protested. "Aren't you supposed to be at the spa?"

"Everyone's gone, thank the stars," Lydia said, scooping towels and sheets and massage table covers out of the basket to add to the piles. "But we're down at least two housekeepers as well, so I'm helping out where I can."

Some of the staff had only been temporary, hired for the duration of the World Mr. Shifter event that had just ended. Travis hadn't expected to lose them so quickly, but Scarlet was nothing if not efficient.

"Did they take the extra staff back to shore in the boat, then?" he asked. "It's on my list to tune up the second engine."

Lydia stared at him. "You haven't heard! Oh, it was

awful — the boat blew up with Tex and Laura in it! They barely made it back with their lives!"

Travis blinked stupidly at her. "I didn't hear about any of that," he said. His gut clenched at the idea of his mate — Tex's mate! He reminded himself — in danger. Also, "They sunk my boat? What about the whale watching tour?"

Lydia laughed, a musical sound. "You slept through quite a story…" she started.

Then the door opened again, this time with Bastian pushing another cart of laundry.

"One of the casters on this thing is off," the dragon shifter said, wiggling the cart to demonstrate. "Aren't you supposed to have the day off, Travis?"

"Aren't you supposed to be on the beach?" Travis countered crossly.

The lifeguard shrugged. "No one is there. One of the girls needed a hand with the laundry."

"I'll fix that," Travis said with a sigh. He kept a basket of extra casters in the back of the laundry room.

"Have you seen Tex this morning?" Bastian asked, with what Travis thought was exaggerated innocence.

Did staring at his mate from across the pool deck count? "Not really," Travis decided to answer, fishing through the basket for the correct caster.

"Had to pull him back to shore on the last sorry piece of your boat," Bastian said. "Guess his mate's friend-of-the-family wasn't such a great friend after all. The Civil Guard has already been here this morning to get him."

Travis stared. If the Civil Guard was involved, there must have been quite a sordid story. "Is that who was trying to kill Miss Smith?" He had to rein in Lynx's out of proportion desire for revenge.

"And her sister!" Lydia exclaimed.

"Though it turns out it was the French housemaid who poisoned her latte," Bastian added, shoveling laundry into the washer until Lydia clucked at him to stop and unpacked the over-stuffed drum.

Feeling very left out, Travis popped the new caster onto the bottom of the cart. "It sounds a pretty far-fetched story."

"Are you coming up to the staff room for dinner?" Lydia asked. "We can catch you up on it."

Travis bit back the question of whether Tex and his mate would be there. It didn't matter; she wasn't his mate.

Is too, Lynx insisted like a child, complete with stomping his big feet.

"I'm not really caught up on my sleep," Travis fibbed. "I'm just going to grab a quiet dinner out of the staff fridge and go to bed early."

He didn't really expect to sleep, given the grip Lynx had on his nerves, but remembering the contents of the fridge made him realize how hungry he was.

He followed Lydia and Bastian carefully out of the laundry, and was relieved to see that the bar was deserted. The sun was already setting, sinking down into the ocean horizon, and Travis was happy to slink away along the path to the staff house by the cliffs.

Breck's cake even sounded pretty good.

Lynx helpfully provided the picture of feeding it, bite by fluffy bite, to his mate. White frosting contrasted against her dark rose lips, and her tongue...

I'm going to give you a cold bath, you filthy tomcat, Travis threatened in return. *That is Tex's mate. Not ours.*

But Lynx's delicious image lingered, despite Travis' best attempts to squelch it.

6

*J*enny stared at the computer screen. It was black, and for a long, confused moment, she had no idea how to go about turning it on.

Before she could confess to the unexpected gap in her knowledge, Scarlet grew impatient and reached over to press the space bar and bring the screen back from sleep.

"I very much appreciated your work with the World Mr. Shifter contract," the red-haired owner said. "Beehag's lawyer is making noises about trying to sell the property out from underneath us again, and I want a better understanding about our lease terms to fight him with."

"Of course," Jenny said faintly.

Scarlet opened the document in question with quick efficient motions on the touchpad while Jenny was still trying to remember what a touchpad was.

After a moment of stillness while Jenny fought down panic, Scarlet added, "I am, of course, happy to pay you your company rates for your time."

Jenny looked blankly at her, then realized that she wasn't going to be able to bluff her way through competence with this. "I'm sorry," she said shrilly. "I... I... can't read it."

The words on the screen might as well have been in a foreign language; Jenny could make no sense of any of it. The letters simply refused to order themselves into any kind of recognizable patterns.

It was a terrifying, helpless feeling, and Jenny was deeply ashamed to admit it.

Scarlet frowned at her, and Jenny told herself it wasn't probably wasn't meant to be a judgmental frown.

"Curious," the resort owner said blandly, giving a little shrug of dismissal. "We can try at another time when you feel up to it."

Jenny got to her feet, trying not to wring her webbed fingers nervously. "I'm so sorry," she said meekly.

Scarlet's expression softened. "I'm sure it will pass," she said kindly. "Your sister is at the bar if you'd like to go see her."

Jenny nodded, and let her feet lead her out of Scarlet's resort-top office and down the white gravel path to the bar. It had just stopped raining, and the sunlight was burning the raindrops off of all the jungle foliage; it smelled clean and delicious.

Laura had a swift hug for her in greeting when Jenny arrived at the bar.

"I'm about to go make up a few of the cottages with fresh laundry," her twin said. "We may or may not be millionaires, but sitting on my ass doesn't suit me, and who knows when we'll actually see any of that."

"Can I help you with it?" Jenny asked.

Laura looked skeptical, but covered it quickly with a smile. "Sure!" she said. "It will go faster with a second set of hands."

Unfortunately, it didn't. Jenny's claws snagged on the

sheets and she was hopelessly clumsy about everything Laura tried to have her help with. Finally, she kept herself to merely sweeping, careful to keep the bristles on the floor so she didn't endanger any of the artwork or vases.

Laura took the time to catch her up. "I talked to Scarlet's contact in a government agency that deals with shifter affairs. His name was Tony, and he was able to get things expedited with getting the charges brought against Fred for killing our parents and withholding our life insurance settlement. I even talked to him about bringing charges against one of the big players in the cartel, Blacksmith — they were already trying to build a case and planning a sting, I guess, and they think my testimony will be enough to make things stick. He said the best thing to do was lie low here until it comes to trial. You'd have a better idea of how that will work than I do."

"I'm — I *was* — a civil lawyer, not a criminal lawyer," Jenny told her, marveling at how competent and self-sufficient Laura had become as she swirled through making beds. "And how did you get mixed up in the mob, anyway?"

"Cartel," Laura corrected. "You know me — I have terrible taste in men and worse judgement when it comes to work. Remember that MLM I lost my savings on?" She tucked a sheet in and pulled it smooth. Clearly, she had done this before, many times; she moved through the housekeeping tasks confidently. "I didn't ask questions I should have until it was too late. Blacksmith paid well in cash and didn't make me fill out a W2."

"As if those weren't warning signs," Jenny scoffed. She immediately felt terrible and judgmental. This was why they always argued as children.

But Laura only chuckled with self-deprecating humor. "It's true," she agreed. "I was an idiot."

"What — what did you do for him?" Jenny wasn't sure she wanted to know.

"Sometimes I carried messages, sometimes I did odd errands. I went to the bank twice a week with a fake ID they gave me and made withdrawals for them. Sometimes they'd have me go to the store and make very exacting purchases. I delivered packages that probably had questionable things in them once or twice."

Jenny sucked her breath in. "Could you get in trouble?"

"Tony doesn't think so. A slap on the wrist at most. Maybe a fine, certainly no jail time. Testifying against Blacksmith could get me off the hook entirely."

Jenny swept her pile out the big double doors onto the deck and off into the tiny lawn below. "You've got everything figured out," she said, as they put the cleaning supplies back and shut the cottage behind them. There was no reason to lock empty buildings here.

Laura took her hand reassuringly, and though Jenny thought she startled at the feeling of the webbing between her fingers, she didn't let go. "You will, too," she said confidently. "I'll help you."

Jenny had to chuckle at how backwards everything seemed to be.

And if she didn't laugh, she'd probably cry.

7

"*A*ren't you supposed to start looking better as you catch up on sleep?" Bastian asked frankly when Travis stumbled down mid-morning.

Travis muttered wordlessly, not wanting to explain that he'd gotten very little in the way of sleep because he couldn't seem to keep from lusting over someone else's mate.

"You do look awful," Breck agreed with Bastian critically.

"Don't you guys have jobs to do?" Travis asked crossly.

"Already done with the breakfast crowd," Breck shrugged.

"I put out the swim-at-your-own-risk sign," Bastian said. "It was raining, earlier. No one was in the water when I left, and I got bored. There's a big storm headed for us, probably hit us in the next few days. I've even heard a bunch of guests have canceled."

Travis went to the fridge with an unappreciative scowl for the waiter and the lifeguard.

"A hurricane?" Breck asked.

"I heard it could be," Bastian said. "They aren't supposed to get as far south as Costa Rica, but it's a category four right now and will still be pretty strong when it hits."

"You guys seen Tex?" Travis had to ask, retreating from the cool sanctuary of the fridge with an egg pastry of some sort and a pile of crispy bacon.

"He's staying with Laura over in cottage six," Bastian explained.

"Mates," Breck said with a shudder. "The horror."

Our mate is close by, Lynx reminded him, as if he hadn't spent the night trying to forget.

Travis made himself eat the suddenly tasteless food, sitting on one of the tall kitchen stools. The house the staff had taken over had a formal dining room, but it had already been converted into a weight and exercise room, sparsely filled with the leftover resort equipment and some rusty hand weights.

Bastian and Breck argued good-naturedly about the boat they wanted to buy to replace the boat that had somehow been sunk the day before — Travis still didn't know the story that went with that, but suspected it was quite a tale.

"What do you think?" Breck asked him abruptly.

Travis shrugged. "I have no opinion one way or the other," seemed like the safest answer, since he hadn't been listening at all.

"That's cheating," Bastian scoffed.

"What are you, Switzerland?" Breck rolled his eyes. "You know you want an inboard this time to run the whale watching tours."

But Travis couldn't focus on the conversation, no matter how invested he was in the outcome. He washed his plate and tossed his napkin.

"What's gotten into you?" Bastian asked, with genuine concern. "Are you okay?"

"I gotta talk to Tex," Travis told him, agonized, and left him more puzzled than ever in his wake.

Tex was sitting on the bar with his guitar, playing something uncharacteristically happy. His mate —

Our mate! purred Lynx.

***His** mate!* Travis corrected in despair.

— sat a few chairs away, a glass of ice water covered with condensing droplets in front of her.

She looked up at his approach, and Travis could see both confusion and longing in her dark eyes.

Travis made the mistake of letting his feet stop, and was still trying to screw together the courage to walk forward again when someone brushed by him.

"Sorry, Travis," she said merrily, and Travis had to stare.

She was a perfect double, dressed in a red sundress compared to her mirror image's blue. She sat between Tex and the other version, and Travis couldn't believe that he had ever confused them. Tex's mate was gorgeous, but his mate —

Our mate! sang Lynx.

— was utterly perfect.

Relief made his knees feel like water. Travis wasn't crazy, it was the world that was crazy. There were two of them, twins, and he was sure he would never have a problem distinguishing them again.

"You alright, man?" Tex asked in concern, stilling his fingers on the strings of the guitar.

Travis could move again, and he strode forward with new confidence. "Never better," he declared. "Though you ladies had me doubting my sanity until now."

Tex's Miss Smith exchanged an amused look with him.

"You didn't know there were two of us?" she asked teasingly.

"I thought I was going to have to skin my own Lynx for insisting that Tex's mate was our own," Travis admitted frankly. "I couldn't imagine a situation more impossible."

"Your mate?! Oh, Jenny, how perfect!" Laura's squeak was nothing but delighted, and Tex grinned congratulations at him.

Jenny only looked alarmed, not at all delighted, but Travis was still buoyed by the revelation that there were two of them.

He closed the distance between them and held out his hands. "My mate," he repeated firmly, almost giddy with relief and joy. "May I kiss you?"

es, her otter insisted. *This is what we want. This is everything!*

The rest of Jenny was in a white-hot panic.

If she let this man kiss her, she would be lost forever to her otter, anything of her human self washed away in the passionate wave of the lust that threatened to consume her. She'd never have any kind of self-control again.

"No!" Jenny said firmly, standing up and pushing her chair back. Instead of sliding, it toppled over backwards with a crash. She was keenly aware of the stares of Tex, her sister, and most of all, of Travis.

He was perfect, she thought achingly. Gorgeous as a model, with golden skin in slanting planes, and shoulders that could carry the world.

He stood before her, hands outstretched, his look of delight and desire fading to confusion and puzzled rejection.

"Jenny," Laura said hesitantly. "What's wrong?"

"What's wrong?" Jenny repeated shrilly. "What's wrong is that I have webbed fingers and sharp teeth, and I can't

eat anything without wanting to dunk it in salt water first."
She heard her voice climb an octave. "What's wrong is that
I've spent nearly two weeks in someone else's skin. What's
wrong is that I can't even read any more, let alone make
sense of words. I don't remember how to turn on a
computer." She turned to Travis. "What's wrong is that
you want to kiss me, and I don't even know you."

We know him, her otter insisted.

"I don't know you," she snarled, and she wasn't sure if
she was replying to her otter, or to Travis, who was gazing
at her as if she were hanging stars instead of having a
ridiculous breakdown.

Rather than continue to stand there looking like an
idiot as she ran out of words, Jenny turned away, and stag-
gered out of the bar, knocking another chair over as she
fled through the tables and out the back entrance.

Half-running, blinded by tears, she ran soundly into
something soft but unyielding, just outside the bar
entrance.

"Gracious, darling! We're on island time, nothing can
be worth a rush like that."

The woman she'd barreled into was as tall as Jenny,
and perhaps three times as wide, rolls of flesh bared at the
shoulders and again at the knees, and otherwise swathed in
swirls of magenta silk. Loose auburn hair hung to her
waist. Despite her soft look, she didn't budge an inch at
Jenny's collision, and if she hadn't put an iron hand at
Jenny's wrist, the fleeing woman would have bounced off
and fallen backwards. Instead, Jenny was steadied on her
feet, and her shoulders were brushed off like an errant
child.

"Oh, sugar, you've been crying," the woman said
compassionately, and even if Jenny hadn't been crying
already, that kindness would have undone her.

As she bawled anew, the woman drew her to a bench in the shade. It creaked alarmingly as they settled on it, and the woman pulled a piece of fabric from an orange beach bag to let Jenny wipe her face.

"Oh," sniffed Jenny as her claws snagged on the fabric. "This is silk... I shouldn't..." She tried to offer it back, tear-stained as it was.

"It will launder," the woman said dismissively, continuing to pat Jenny's shoulder in comfort. "Or it won't, no matter. What does matter is that you look like you've lost your best friend, and here we are at a beautiful resort where you ought to be enjoying the good food and good views." She put a hand at Jenny's chin and tipped it up to look into her eyes.

Were they human eyes this time? Or were they her otter's dark eyes with no whites?

Whatever the woman found there, Jenny forced herself to look steadily back. She had the most arresting violet-blue eyes.

"I'm Magnolia," the woman said, smiling and releasing her chin. "And that's a little better now, isn't it. Sometimes a good cry is just what you need to put things back into perspective."

"I'm Jenny, and I'm sorry to bother you," Jenny said, wiping away the last tears from her face. "I'm just... a little new to being a shifter." It seemed like the simplest explanation.

"Ah," Magnolia nodded. "That doesn't happen often, but I imagine it's quite an upset. Particularly if you think you have your life all figured out in a particular way."

Jenny stared. Was that why she was having so much trouble? She had been so sure about the path of her life. She was going to be the best lawyer, the best... sister.

Now, here she was, unsure of everything, right down to

the shape of her body and the direction of her heart. Her sister was *better* than her, at *everything*, and Jenny was unexpectedly the one falling apart.

"Believe me, darling," Magnolia was saying, "I grew up on a very different island than this, and thought my life would play out in a very different way. But I chose differently, and haven't looked back, and you'll figure out the best path for yourself, too."

Without revulsion, Magnolia picked up one of Jenny's misshapen hands. "You may not be used to all the new features, but don't forget for a moment that you are the beautiful sum all your parts."

Jenny wished she had a fraction of the confidence the big woman exuded. "Thank you," she said genuinely. She couldn't consider the claws or the webbing beautiful, but she tried to remember that becoming an otter *had* saved her life.

"Oh honey," the big woman said cheerfully, "You are as welcome as the dawn! Now, it's been two weeks since I had one of Tex's margarita's, and that is two weeks too many." She heaved to her feet, tucking the silk Jenny had cried on back into her big orange beach bag.

"Jenny! Oh, Magnolia, you're back!"

Jenny turned at Gizelle's cheerful call.

"Gizelle, honey!" Magnolia opened her arms, and Gizelle darted in and gave her a swift hug. "You're getting brave, darling," Magnolia told her proudly.

"There were so many people," Gizelle told her frankly. "It was noisy and smelly while you were gone. But I didn't break anything and I only shifted…" she counted silently on her fingers until she ran out.

"That's excellent," Magnolia told her before she could finish. From anyone else it might have sounded patronizing, but Jenny felt like it was genuine and gracious. "And you've met Jenny."

"She's a *twin*," Gizelle said, as if Jenny wasn't standing right there. "I'm *helping* her. She *needs* it."

"That's lovely of you, sugar," Magnolia said with an amused sideways look at Jenny.

Jenny wasn't sure if she should feel insulted or not, but decided she mostly felt touched by Gizelle's attention and Magnolia's kindness.

Gizelle took Jenny's hand, not appearing to notice Jenny's reluctance to give it to her. She didn't flinch at the claws or webbing. "I want to practice shifting with you before dinner," she said commandingly. "I'm *good* at it."

"You enjoy that," Magnolia said with a wave over her shoulder. "I'm off to the pool deck for the rest of the afternoon! I've missed the sunshine!"

Jenny let Gizelle lead her in the opposite direction. Perhaps shifting would take her mind off of the memory of Travis' heartbroken face while she decided what she was going to do about him.

It's not what we're going to do about him, her otter told her slyly. *It's what we're going to do **with** him.*

9

In the wake of Jenny's stormy exit, Travis bent down slowly and picked up the chair she had toppled over. He put it carefully back in place on its feet, keenly aware of the presence of Tex and Laura, and the absence of his mate.

"Well," Tex said, full of false cheer, "that didn't go quite the way I expected it to."

"I'm sorry," Laura said, more sincerely. "She's going through a lot right now, of course."

"Of course," Travis agreed numbly. Lynx was pacing miserably in his head.

There was a moment of awkward silence, broken by the arrival of Graham, the lion shifter in charge of the grounds. It was odd that his entrance was the loudest thing in the room; he was as quiet as always.

Graham cleared his throat, looking from one uncomfortable person to another. "Storm hitting in a few days. Scarlet's got me shuttering the cottages that aren't being used," he said gruffly. "Said Travis might have some thoughts on electrical things that need extra protection."

"I'll come with you," Travis said, glad for the distraction. He picked up his toolbox and went for the stairs down. "Start at the bottom and work up?"

Graham gave one last suspicious look at Tex and Laura, then shrugged and answered by following Travis, his machete over a shoulder.

Graham was exactly the company Travis would have chosen for this task; he kept conversation to exactly what was necessary and no more.

The cottages were not built for strong winds; such weather rarely came to the island. Graham and Travis moved all the outdoor furniture and decoration into each cottage and made sure every door and window was latched securely, moving anything fragile back from windows that might get blown out.

Travis turned off the meters at each cottage, so no power would be running through them, and had Graham help him pull down a few solar panels in more precarious positions. He checked outdoor lights for stability, and screwed a few fixtures in more tightly.

Graham scanned the greenery as well, and judiciously took down branches overhanging the cottages that looked like they were a breakage risk.

Travis thought he muttered as he made every cut, and as they left the last cottage, asked curiously, "How'd you end up here, Graham?"

Graham had been the only other employee at Shifting Sands when Travis had started, though it hadn't been long before Bastian and Breck had been hired. A series of cooks had been fired in short succession before Chef arrived with Magnolia. Getting her to stay on as a long-term resident had been a coup for the kitchen, because Chef wouldn't have stayed without her, and he had proved to be a genius at food preparation, earning his nickname within a week.

Graham was quiet for so long that Travis had stopped expecting an answer. Then the gardener finally shrugged and volunteered, "Got a letter from Scarlet. Seemed like a better option than any of my others." He didn't elaborate about those previous options, but Travis wondered, as he had several times before, if there was a slight British accent to his words; he didn't sound *entirely* American.

"You?"

Graham's query was a surprise. He rarely pursued conversation, if he could be coaxed into it at all.

"Grew up in a Native village in the middle of nowhere, Alaska," Travis said briefly. "Went to the city to get my certifications, but cities don't really suit me. I saw an employment ad in an underground shifter magazine I subscribed to and it sounded like a nice change of pace. I sent a resume, and got a letter back inviting me out. It was supposed to be temporary, but Scarlet never ran out of work, and I honestly can't imagine living somewhere else now."

Could he? Jenny must have had a life established in California, maybe she was planning to return to it.

We would follow her, Lynx assured him, even though they both shuddered at the idea of a crowded Californian city.

Graham grunted, slicing down an overhanging branch efficiently and hauling it back out of the way into the hedge. Travis knew that their brief moment of conversation had ended. He finished the last power disconnect, and double-checked the latch on the door.

Whatever the storm brought the next evening, Travis was fairly certain that the resort was ready for it.

Whatever his mate brought, he'd be ready for that, as well.

10

*J*enny wondered if Gizelle had forgotten about her. The tiny woman had demonstrated a shift into her gazelle form, then wandered away to nibble on the grass without a backwards glance. Currently, she was grazing earnestly across the little lawn where they had been meeting every day, ostensibly for Jenny to practice shifting.

Most days, Gizelle had Jenny shift several times, repeating her advice about thinking *as* the form she was aiming for, not *about* the form she was aiming for. Jenny's shifts had grown less painful, but she still dreaded them, and she was still never fully human.

This time, her fingers had no webbing, but the short, no-nonsense claws at the ends pressed little divets into her palms when she clenched her fists.

Jenny sighed and lay back in the prickly grass, looking up into sky. It was blue and clear, and the sun beat down with even more strength than the Californian sun. There wasn't the slightest hint of a breeze, and the early afternoon was sweltering. Jenny fanned the bottom of her sundress to cool her sweaty legs. Maybe she should bring a lawn chair out with her next time; the grass prickled distractingly at her skin, making her think of her otter's coarse fur.

She wondered if lynx fur was softer, and suspected it was. Laura had told her everything she knew about Travis, without Jenny asking. Her sister was clearly more excited about her mate than Jenny was, and seemed puzzled that Jenny was still trying to avoid him.

It wasn't that she didn't want him; she couldn't sleep at night without imagining him beside her. She fantasized about touching his golden-brown skin, running fingers through his short, thick hair, had to try to keep her mind from wandering to still dirtier topics.

Abruptly, there was a big deer-like face right above her, blocking the sunlight. Spiraled horns curving dangerously back from between her bell-like ears.

Gizelle snuffled at her, then shifted like mercury into her human form, crouching beside Jenny. "Are you napping?" She was so close that her long, wild hair tickled Jenny, and she didn't move back much when Jenny sat upright. She had an odd sense of personal space, Jenny had found, sometimes so close that it was uncomfortable, sometimes keeping so much space between them that conversation was awkward.

"No, I'm not napping," Jenny assured her, though she'd been comfortable enough that she might have.

"Oh good! Let's practice!"

Gizelle jumped to her feet in one fluid move, while Jenny stood up more carefully.

"Go!" Gizelle commanded, startling Jenny.

She shifted obediently, braced for the discomfort, and a few moments later was shaking off the last of the pain and scampering on four small feet in grass that suddenly seemed very tall.

A fleet-footed gazelle danced easily with her, leaping high into the air, then stomped an imperious foot and was standing as a human.

Jenny drew a deep breath into her capable otter lungs and tried to keep Gizelle's advice in mind. She thought about what it was like to be a human, how much taller she was, focusing on fingers without webbing or claws. She remembered what it was like to type on a computer keyboard, how long and nimble her hands could be. She ignored her otter, who scoffed and protested that otter fingers were just as clever.

Then she was panting with the effort and looking in triumph at her fingers.

They were her fingers again, free from each other and with her old familiar short fingernails.

"I did it," Jenny gasped, feeling exhausted with the effort. "I did it!"

Gizelle was looking at her curiously. "I... suppose," she said reluctantly.

"I feel like I ran a marathon," Jenny confessed, feeling a little deflated by Gizelle's lack of enthusiasm.

"It shouldn't be that hard," Gizelle said. "Can't you feel the power around you to shift with?"

"Power?"

Gizelle put on what Jenny was recognizing as her teacher face. "It takes energy to shift, of course. But it shouldn't have to come from your own reserves. There is power all around you to draw on, just reach out and use it whenever you need. You should only have to focus."

Was that a feature of all places, Jenny wondered, or just this particular strange island?

Gizelle continued, her expression growing distant and

her voice taking on a sing-song tone. "There are wells of power that make the sunless sky, and they can make prison walls or set you free with the right key. Drink it down and you can taste the future and touch the chains that hold the world together…"

Jenny watched her with concern. "Gizelle?" She asked tentatively, hoping to distract her from the trance she was in.

Gizelle ignored her. "Voices of power. Spells set in violence and chaos. Prisons. Things that shouldn't be disturbed…"

Sometimes Gizelle seemed normal enough that it was easy to forget that she had spent many of her formative years imprisoned and forced to remain in her animal form. And then there were these fugue states, when she ceased to make sense. It was hypnotic, sometimes more than just figuratively. Jenny reached up to pinch her neck and keep from falling into the spell with her.

The side of her face exploded in sensation, and Jenny flinched away in alarm and surprise, yelping out loud.

"What?" Gizelle asked, puzzled, but back in reality with her.

Jenny reached a cautious hand up towards her face. "I felt… something."

Stiff, flexible fibers met her fingertips, and the barest brush sent a battery of sensory input to her face.

"Whiskers?!" Jenny shrieked. "I have whiskers!"

These weren't a grandmother's mustache-like whiskers, they were inches-long, and bristled out from her face like quivering array of antennae.

Gizelle shrugged dismissively. "They look lovely," she promised, but Jenny could picture what she looked like quite clearly and knew better.

In her head, her otter was holding her sides and rolling with laughter.

Jenny gritted her teeth. "Let's practice some more," she ground out, even though she was still tired from the last shift.

Gizelle shrugged, obviously mystified by her discomfort. "We can do it some more," she agreed.

"Until I'm me," Jenny declared. "*Just* me."

Good luck with that, her otter teased.

11

"*W*ant something stronger in your orange juice?" Tex offered. He was hauling trash bags in one hand and a milk crate stuffed with gathered glass bottles in the other.

The bar was empty and Travis was alone. Only two guests were in sight, both of them on the pool deck below.

Magnolia was lounging on one of the chairs by the pool, soaking up the last rays of the late afternoon sun, a margarita in hand.

The other guest was a thickly built man with short-cropped dark hair who looked uncomfortable lounging in his deck chair. He wore mirrored sunglasses and was reading a paperback novel. A bottle of water was gathering condensation on the table next to him.

Travis considered the drink Tex was offering, but finally shook his head. He had a feeling that if he started drinking, he wasn't going to want to stop. His heart hurt for his bewildered mate, and Lynx was yowling and pacing inside of him.

He settled for saying, "Nah."

Tex shrugged. "Suit yourself!" He returned to cleaning and emptying bins.

Travis couldn't get Jenny's face out of his head, and the lost, frightened look made him ball his hands into fists and want to fight something. But there was nothing to fight, and she didn't want his help. She had successfully evaded him for several days now.

There was nothing critical left to fix. The resort was as ready for the storm coming as he could make it. Everything was running perfectly smoothly. Even the heaps of laundry had finally been finished, and the big machines were still again.

When he looked up and saw Scarlet walking up from the pool deck, it seemed like perfect timing.

"What do you need?" he asked too eagerly. "What's next on the renovation schedule?"

Scarlet frowned at him. "You've done a lot of work these last few weeks, you do deserve some time off."

Travis frowned back, trying to figure out how to explain that he needed something to keep his hands busy while his newly-a-shifter mate decided what to do with him. Scarlet wouldn't appreciate an emotional confession or a rambling story about mistaken identity, and she wasn't the sort of person who invited intimacy.

Finally, he stuck with the simplest answer. "I don't really want any time off."

Scarlet gave him an appraising look and went to the bar. She came back to his table with one of the resort brochures. "We're going to have to get these updated with cottage numbers on the ones we put back into service," she said thoughtfully, spreading it out between them. "And we'll take the whale watching note off until we can get another boat."

Travis leaned over the colorful map. "Cottage five could use an upgrade to the bathroom and new windows."

Scarlet made a discouraging noise. "As busy as we were last week, we are not rolling in money. We have a boat that the insurance doesn't want to replace, we lost an entire shipment of groceries, and the air conditioner in the hotel was supposed to be a priority." She didn't have to add that several of the months before that had been in the red as the resort hosted dozens of refugees from a lunatic's shifter zoo on the other side of the island.

"What about the deck at cottage twelve?" Travis suggested, tapping it on the map. "It's got enough rotten decking to be a hazard as it is now, and we've got a bunch of treated lumber leftover from our last deck job. It should be enough to redo it."

Scarlet nodded. "That's an excellent plan."

"There's enough spare tile left to retile the bathroom in cottage five, even if we don't put in new fixtures," Travis suggested, knowing that the deck would only be a morning's worth of work.

"Let's do that, too," Scarlet agreed. "Be aware that there is a storm due to hit the island tomorrow evening. We almost never get hurricanes this far south, but it's still a category three and doesn't appear to be slowing down like usual. We should shutter up the cottages that aren't in use, and we should be prepared to stage repairs afterwards."

Travis nodded. "Already done. Bastian told me about the storm this morning, so I made sure all the cottages not occupied got shuttered and we've got some spare roof tile if we need it afterwards."

Scarlet looked pleased, with a slight, approving smile and a nod. "Excellent. We won't have many guests to worry about—"

She continued to say something else, but Travis could

make no sense out of her words, because Lynx clenched claws into his heart just then, and he looked up to find Jenny watching them.

She was standing in the back of the bar, arms folded across her bountiful breasts. The royal blue sundress swished around her knees and left her perfect shoulders bare. She was still tucked up, like she was trying to hold herself in, but Travis thought her gaze was steadier, more sure. The sun was beginning its evening plunge into the sea, and the color of the light made her glow

He was warring with himself, trying to decide if it was better to give her space or give in to Lynx's desire to pounce now, while she was within reach.

Scarlet's sigh of disgust as she rose made Travis look around at her in embarrassment.

"There's no rush on any of those improvements," she told him with a single raised eyebrow, and then she clicked away in her short heels towards the back entrance, giving Jenny a brief nod of greeting as they passed.

Then his mate was strolling towards him, and Travis felt his breath stop at the beauty of her grace.

12

*J*enny told herself she wasn't going to the bar to find Travis, she was going to find Laura, but she somehow wasn't surprised or disappointed to find her mate instead of her sister.

He was sitting with Scarlet in the setting sun, looking at a brochure spread out between them. The sunset colors made the owner's hair look like it was aflame, but Jenny was captured by Travis, looking seriously over the map. His face was drawn into concentration, and while she watched, he dragged a hand through his short, tousled hair. The play of golden light over his muscles made Jenny draw in a breath and fold her arms tighter across her chest.

Then he looked up, and the way his face lit up hit Jenny in the gut.

Whether she was ready or not, whether she deserved him or not, they were destined for each other. This was the man she was perfectly made for.

And it terrified her.

She made herself unclench her fists, glad at least that she and Gizelle had practiced shifting until she could be human without webbed fingers. The claws were still there, and the pointed teeth, and one of the practice shifts she'd had stiff whiskers protruding from her cheeks. But she knew that Travis wouldn't care about that, and it was oddly comforting to know.

Scarlet rose then, and passed Jenny with a cool nod of greeting, leaving them alone on the deck above the pool.

Jenny made her feet move, and her otter was wriggling in delight as they closed the distance to their mate.

He stood as she approached, and Jenny had to tip her head back to look up into his face.

"I wondered if you'd like to... take a walk."

It wasn't what her otter wanted to suggest, but it was a step Jenny was willing to make.

Travis gazed down at her with adoration that made Jenny squirm uncomfortably, then he cleared his throat and said politely, "That would be lovely."

He pivoted and offered Jenny his arm, which she took, shivering at the touch of his flesh under her fingers.

"Have you seen the gardens?" He asked with a gruff tone that made Jenny suspect that he was as affected by the touch of her skin as she was.

Jenny shook her head, not trusting her own voice.

Travis swallowed. "Would you like to?"

Jenny nodded wordlessly, and he led her out the back entrance of the bar to a gravel path that she had never taken.

Paths she hadn't taken was a theme that seemed to apply to a lot of her life lately.

The evening was a tapestry of purple and magenta, sparkled with stars. The garden was well enough away from the brightly-lit main areas of the resort that it was dark enough to see the features of the moonless sky, framed in the jungle trees that edged the garden.

Jenny marveled at her otter's night vision. If she weren't so busy resenting the otter's constant voice and unwelcome features, there were parts to being a shifter that she could grow to like.

She paused at a vine of white flowers that were climbing riotously up a trellis and reached for one of the blooms.

"Don't pick them," Travis warned.

Jenny froze. "Poisonous?" she asked.

Travis' laugh was her new favorite sound, and her otter practically did backflips of joy over it. "No, Graham is just really, really protective of his gardens. I wouldn't let him hurt you, but I'm not entirely convinced I would win in a fistfight."

Jenny glanced over at him, letting her eyes linger over the muscles under his polo shirt. She couldn't imagine that anyone would be able to beat him in a fistfight. He was not only broad-shouldered and strong, but he moved with a grace and efficiency of motion that made Jenny suspect he was underestimating his own proficiency.

Either way, she didn't want to be the cause of any more trouble at the resort than she already had been. She left the flower unmolested.

There was a bench tucked into one corner under a violet-flowered shrub, and they sat together. It was a small enough bench that Travis' thigh was against Jenny's, and she was keenly aware of how badly she wanted to have less clothing between them even than her thin skirt and his mid-weight khakis.

"I never meant to cause you discomfort," Travis said, awkwardly clearing his throat.

Jenny put an automatic hand on his thigh. "It wasn't you," she said, realizing how trite it sounded. "It was all me. I was... I am... in a really weird place. I don't want you to think I'm not... ah... interested."

"I'll be patient," Travis told her sincerely. "I'll make Lynx be patient."

"No promises about my otter," Jenny laughed weakly. "I don't think patience is her strong suit."

Something occurred to her. "You say 'Lynx' like it's capitalized. Not 'my lynx,' or 'a lynx,' but 'Lynx.' I haven't heard any other shifters say it like that."

"I grew up in a native village in Alaska, and our shifter lore goes back to old stories, about times when Lynx and Raven and Bear were spirits that roamed the world in their own skins."

Travis' voice caught a little as he spoke and Jenny realized that she had unconsciously started caressing his thigh.

Down girl, she told her otter, making her hand still. She wasn't quite willing to remove it.

"So you think of it as a spirit animal, or a totem?"

"Essentially, yes," Travis said.

Somehow, when she thought of her otter, it was too frivolous to be considered a serious totem animal.

One of us has to not take themselves too seriously, her otter replied with a sniff.

"Tell me about growing up in Alaska," Jenny said wistfully.

"I lived in a tiny village near the Brooks Range," Travis said. "You've never seen a land so beautiful and harsh. The summers are full of light and mosquitoes, the winters are endless twilight and cold so sharp it makes your nose hairs frost." He carefully covered her hand with his own, lacing his fingers into hers. She was glad the webbing hadn't come out in this shift.

Jenny and her otter both listened, enthralled, as Travis talked about a world so different from the mild-climate city life that Jenny had grown up in. His tales about the winter were an odd contrast to the warm, fragrant darkness they sat in now.

"Tell me about California," Travis suggested then.

Hesitantly, Jenny talked about growing up in the city-sprawl of Southern California. "I looked up to my dad so much. I always wanted to be a lawyer like he was. It was my whole goal in life."

"You must be pretty good at it," Travis said. "Laura said you were offered a partnership."

Jenny shrugged. "I'm not sure. I mean, I worked hard, but maybe it was just because my dad had been a partner…"

"I don't know much about law," Travis said, richly skeptical, "but I'm pretty sure they don't give partnerships just for your genes. Have you ever heard of imposter syndrome?"

"Yes, of course," Jenny said with a crooked smile she belatedly realized Travis couldn't see. "And yes, guilty." Thoughtfully, she added, "I feel like an imposter as a lawyer, *and* as a shifter."

"Give yourself time," Travis said. "You've only been a shifter a few days, really." He touched the side of her face tenderly, and Jenny wondered if he could see in the dark, too. It would make sense. His fingertips made her skin tingle.

Abruptly, Jenny decided it was time to be brave. "Earlier, you asked if you could kiss me," she said, voice hoarse.

He froze beside her, and Jenny could feel his coiled attention. Her otter was aquiver with anticipation.

"Even though my otter wanted to say yes, I was afraid. I was afraid there wouldn't be anything left of me if I did."

"I understand," Travis said, and Jenny could feel him fighting down disappointment. Was this what being a mate was like, more sure of his emotions than she was of her own? Could he sense her otter wriggling in need and lust the way she could sense his lynx? Did he think she was going to fight the creature instinct down again?

"I'm not afraid anymore," she said quietly. "We both want you to kiss us."

She ran a nervous tongue over her sharp teeth and swallowed. She knew he still wanted to, but would he like what he found?

13

*T*ravis didn't need a second invitation.

With one smooth motion, he was gathering Jenny into his arms, and drawing her mouth to his for a kiss.

She gave a little whimper as she opened her mouth to him, hot and willing, and Travis dove in to claim it for his own.

Sharp teeth met questing tongue, and it only heightened his heat and desire. He slipped a hand along her neck, using his other arm to pull her close, kissing her with all his strength and focus.

"Oh, Travis," she said, when he released her and she could catch her breath. "I… didn't know it could be like that."

"It can be more," Travis said, sliding both hands up to cradle her face.

This time when he kissed her, it was more slowly, more demandingly, and he didn't release her until she was wordlessly begging for more, writhing against him wantonly.

Was that her otter, or was it his Jenny? Was there any difference now?

Ours, Lynx purred.

He reached down and slid on hand up under her dress, cupping the outside of one thigh, one tantalizing ass cheek, and then found the thin fabric of her underwear.

He paused with one finger at the edge of the garment, giving her a chance to change her mind or draw away, and she whined and pressed closer in unmistakable invitation.

He drew it off of her, lifting her into his lap in one smooth motion. There was no way that she wouldn't realize now how badly he wanted her; he was harder than he'd ever been, and the fabric of his pants did little to hold his member down.

She gyrated on him, making him groan in need and desire, and Travis had to concentrate to keep from tearing her dress in eagerness as he slipped it off over her head.

She was not so gentle with him, and Travis heard a seam of his polo shirt rip as she clawed it off of him, kissing him hungrily whenever undressing gave them the opportunity.

"Pants," she said, breathing hard. Travis thought it was a slang expression of disgust, then realized she was actually concerned about his pants, fumbling with the button and belt. Travis stood, lifting her with him, and she gave a little gasp, giggling and grabbing around his neck.

Gently, he lay her down in a bed of flowers, kissing down her neck and arms as she reluctantly let go of him. He had never removed his pants so swiftly, returning to straddle her. She wore only her bra now, and it was everything that Travis could do not to simply let Lynx rut as he wished.

She wants us, Lynx insisted.

We can be a better lover than that, Travis countered.

So instead of burying himself inside her the way he so desperately wanted, he slipped a questing finger into her treasure.

She arched up to his hand, crying in pleasure and begging for release. He added a second finger, thrusting into her gently, slowly, making her squirm and gasp and snap her teeth in need. Her hands on his shoulders scratched and clawed, and when he coaxed a release from her, she sank her short claws reflexively into him.

"Oh!" She said in alarm, as the waves of pleasure ebbed away and Travis slowed his thrusting fingers in time with her breaths. "I must have hurt you!"

"It isn't pain," Travis assured her, and it wasn't. It was only sensation, glorious contact with his mate and an expression of his ability to make her resonate.

But he wasn't able to hold back his own need now, and when he pressed his hungry cock against her, she opened her legs eagerly.

She was so wet, so soaked in her own joyous juices, that Travis slipped in faster than he meant to, driving into her to the base of his shaft in one firm motion.

She cried out in ecstasy, rising to meet him and wrap her legs around his waist. "Yes, oh, yes," she gasped.

Her encouragement was all that Travis needed to begin thrusting in earnest, losing himself in the velvet of her skin, the smell of her sex, the sounds of her enjoyment. When she came again, clawing more gently along his arms this time, he made himself withdraw, panting and fighting hard not to come too quickly himself. He gently pulled her up, kissing her, then guided her over onto her knees.

She was intoxicatingly responsive, finding fresh delight in this new angle of penetration, and Travis finally let himself empty into her, his finally shuddering thrusts making her cry out in release one final time.

14

*J*enny didn't realize she was dozing until Travis stirred beside her and she jolted into awareness again.

The delicious languor of sex still felt like it was weighing down her limbs, but familiar doubts were resurfacing. Was this connection all otter and none of her own self? Would she continue to feel less human if she let herself fall further in love with this man?

The smell of crushed greens penetrated her thoughts, and Jenny realized that they were lying in one of the flower beds. She was delightfully sore in unexpected places, and felt guilty.

"Is Graham going to be angry?" she asked tentatively.

"Screw Graham," Travis said, drawing her closer into his arms.

Jenny chuckled into his shoulder.

"I should go," she said, finally pulling away and sitting up. "Once I find my clothes."

Travis sat up beside her, a hand on her thigh, caressing her gently in a way that made her blood stir even after all they'd already done. "I have a room in the staff house at the edge of the resort. You can stay the night there with me."

Jenny didn't want to admit that she had spent the night before as an otter. She found it impossible to sleep as a human, her thoughts too jumbled up and chaotic to give her any rest. Only slipping back into otter form had brought her peace, and she'd slept in a pile of leaves under a hedge. Gizelle assumed she slept nights at Laura's cottage, and Laura still thought she was rooming with Gizelle. Wherever that was.

"I... can't," she said, drawing away and scrambling to her feet. She found her dress with one foot, and yanked it over her head with determination. Her sandals were next to the bench, and she stuffed her feet into them.

Travis rose from the flower garden, a gorgeous slab of naked hunk even in the very faint, shivery light of stars and distant resort lights. "Jenny..."

This was the 'what happens next' talk, Jenny realized, and panic rose up in her throat, choking her. She didn't know *what* she wanted, even if she was now sure *who* she wanted. This was too fast, too much, it was all otter, not herself. She didn't know who she was.

"I'm sorry," she squeaked, and then she fled, not even bothering to find her underwear.

You're going the wrong direction! her otter told her shrilly.

Jenny stumbled over the path, her vision swimming as she battled otter inside her head for control over her limbs.

I didn't ask for you, she wailed at the creature in her head.

You needed me, the otter returned, fiercely.

You can't hold that against me forever, Jenny protested. *You saved me, great. But I want my life back.*

I'm not trying to hold anything against you, her otter growled back. *But I clearly haven't finished saving you. You still need me.*

I need you? Jenny was outraged. *I need you like I need a hole in the head. You want nothing but pleasures of the flesh, pursuing your own selfish agendas. You don't even care that you've ruined my life. I can't do my job! I can't read! I can't shift without claws, or whiskers, or pointed teeth because you won't let go of me!*

She thought that the silence in response was a victory, but her otter finally came back and told her softly, *Did you ever think that you can't shift completely human because you're afraid of losing me, that it's **you** not letting go of **me**?*

Jenny's feet had taken her inexorably to the ocean, and she stood at the edge of the deserted beach now and considered her otter's uncomfortable idea without flinching. The chairs were all folded up and leaning against the beach bar. The stretch of empty sand was silver, with faint gossamer waves lapping against the shore. A sign proclaimed that no lifeguard was on duty.

She slipped off her sandals, and after a moment, her dress and bra, folding them neatly.

See? her otter gloated. *Naked is more fun.*

Jenny stepped into the sand, feeling the grains sift up between her toes like doubts. Was it true? Was she just afraid of being alone again?

She walked out to the edge of the water and turned to look back. The resort rose above her like a castle. Only the bar deck and a few stray windows were lit, and the underwater lights of the pool gave the underside of the palm trees an unearthly glow. Darkness undoubtedly hid her from anyone who might have been watching.

Jenny turned back to the ocean. She'd spent weeks out in that dark water, always an otter, always only barely aware of who she'd been. She waded out, feeling the pull of the waves at her ankles, then her knees. Sand slipped out from beneath her feet with the power of the water. Then she was swimming, with human arms and legs for the first time since her otter had come to her, and she sucked in a breath and dove under, eyes closed.

Water embraced her, and she felt the rush of the gentle currents around her. She drove forward, memorizing the feeling of her muscles with each stroke, the way her body moved when it was surrounded by water. She had to smile at the soreness that Travis had left her, and she broke the surface with a gasp for breath before breaking into an easy stroke along the surface, swimming out into the ocean.

It felt odd, after so much swimming as her otter. In some ways, she was comparatively awkward, not at all the lithe, graceful creature her furry alter-ego was. But in some ways, she was more beautiful as a human.

It was odd to find her otter in her head, enjoying the swimming as much as she was, reveling in the differences between them.

We're different, her otter told her, unexpectedly kind. *I'm not better*.

Jenny sighed. *I'm… sorry*, she told her. *I haven't been very understanding*.

She drew in a deep breath, dove under the water, and shifted.

It was a painless shift, executed between one breath and the time she would have wanted another, and she was the small, agile otter again, diving joyfully through the water.

The shift back was just as painless and smooth, and Jenny was breaking the surface and exhaling her stale air to take another breath. She didn't have to check to know that her teeth were only human-sharp, and that her fingers had no claws or webbing.

She rolled to her back, an otter motion that was less easily achieved by her human form.

I am better at that, otter scoffed, then added sweetly, *but you'll improve.*

I think you have always been in my head, Jenny mused. *You are every bad idea I ever ignored.*

*Maybe **you've** been every bad idea **I've** ever ignored,* her otter told her merrily in return.

Jenny chuckled, arms wide as she bobbed at the surface of the water.

I still don't know what to do about Travis, she said, after a moment of serene floating.

We'll figure it out, her otter told her carelessly. *He is our mate, and he'll be patient while you work through your issues.*

Jenny had to laugh. *It's like having the most unsympathetic psychiatrist in the world in my head with me,* she said wryly.

15

"*I*t's insane," Travis admitted. "I'm on the world's worst roller coaster. Or the best, I can't decide." It was early enough that the sun wasn't up yet, but most of the staff was already getting ready for the day, gathered informally in the dated kitchen for breakfast.

"Yeah," Tex agreed with a drawl, leaning past him to get into the refrigerator. "Stick it out, man. She'll be worth the lows getting there. Her sister sure is." He shared a sly sideways grin as he came out of the fridge with a piece of pizza.

It wasn't often that the resort had such a pedestrian offering, and of course, it was a pizza with Chef's special flare: a mild, herby sauce with chopped basil, olives, and sausage crumbles, all smothered in white cheeses. Breck had brought all of the leftover pieces from the night before when he'd closed the dining hall.

Travis considered a piece for himself, but wasn't sure he wanted breakfast at all. Jenny had vanished after their evening tryst, and as much as he wanted to hunt her down and repeat the event, he knew he had to give her whatever space she needed. His chest hurt, and he was sure that food wouldn't fill the emptiness that her absence left in him.

"Guh," Breck disagreed vehemently. "Mates. Run while you can."

"You can't run from your mate," Tex told him. "And believe me, you won't want to."

"Oh, I can," Breck scoffed. "And believe me, I will." He elbowed past Travis, who was still camped out next to the fridge, and got his own piece of pizza.

"Breck finding his mate is going to be a train-wreck," Bastian observed, yawning his way into the kitchen. "Close your robe, Breck. No one wants to see that."

"Plenty of people want to see that," Breck smirked and leaned back against the counter as he ate, making sure the robe gaped just right. "This place *is* clothing optional."

"The *resort* is clothing optional," Bastian argued. "Not the staff house." He edged past Breck distastefully and moved Travis aside to grab two pieces of Chef's pizza out the fridge.

"I'm with Bastian," Tex agreed. "We need house rules that include a dress code."

"No Speedos," Bastian suggested. "Shoes off at the door."

"No nudity," Tex added.

"No cowboy hats," Breck countered.

"Hey now," Tex protested. "That's pretty specific."

"So is the nudity clause." Breck went for another slice of the pizza, making Travis realize that he was still standing too close to the door. He sighed, and got his own slice before the fridge door swung closed.

"There are more than two hundred guest beds in this resort," Graham announced, coming into the kitchen like a storm cloud.

The staff looked at him expectantly, and Travis looked

up from taking the first bite of Chef's pizza-like delicacy to find that the brunt of Graham's glare was for him.

"And you had to use a *flower bed*?" Graham finished, biting off every word like it was dirty.

Breck, Tex, and Bastian all drew in theatrical breathes.

"Oh snap," Breck said. "See, I told you mates were trouble."

"You've smashed your share of flower beds," Tex reminded him.

"Hush," Breck said. "Travis is in trouble right now."

Travis made a sound that might have been a growl and might have been clearing his throat. "Sorry about the garden," he said, not feeling particularly sorry.

Graham stalked towards Travis, giving him a moment of concern, but opened the refrigerator instead, surveying the options before deciding on the last slice of the pizza.

He gave Travis a look chillier than the air escaping from the fridge and swept back out without another word.

"Dodged a bullet," Bastian laughed.

"I'm just glad we don't have to clean up any blood this time," Breck said, sounding faintly disappointed.

"Thanks for all the backup," Travis said sarcastically.

"No problem," Tex said cheerfully, clapping him on the back.

Travis left the house muttering, toolbox in hand, but he was smiling wryly.

The first thing he did was tear up the old decking from the porch at cottage twelve. It was cathartic to destroy it down to the structure, ripping up the previous boards with a crowbar or just his own hands. The next thing was to carry the new boards down from the other job site. With the bar still closed for the morning, Tex helped him haul them down.

"If I see Jenny, I'll tell her where you are," the bartender promised.

"Thanks," Travis told him, then lost himself in setting up the job site, leveling the sawhorses, and running the extension cord for the chop saw and the hose from the compressor.

He felt Jenny before he saw her, the hair at the back of his neck rising to attention as Lynx began to caper in eagerness.

Turning to see her was like a shock of electricity. She looked fresh and well-rested, and so breathtakingly gorgeous that Travis had to shift his hips to give his growing member space in his pants.

"Don't let me interrupt you," she said shyly. "I was just… looking for something to do. Some way to help."

Travis could think of something to do, but knew it wasn't what she meant. "I'd love your help."

She walked hesitantly into the work site, skirting around the chop saw cautiously. "I'm not sure how helpful I'll be. I'm… still having trouble reading words."

"Numbers, too?" Travis asked. He handed her a tape measure and noticed that her fingers had short, sensible nails, not claws.

She unrolled it a few inches and shrugged. "Apparently, I can read numbers."

Travis gave her ear protection and showed her how to hook the end of the tape measure on a board and mark the right number. "This porch is an easy job," he said. "All the boards will be exactly the same length. Some jobs, it's as much measuring as it is anything else; it can be tricky when every piece is a new length." He showed her how to place a speed-square and mark a line across the board. It was distracting, being so close to her delicious smell. He wanted to caress her, but kept his touches professional, even if he couldn't keep his lingering glances quite as reserved.

He caught more than one appraising glance in return, and several times, she licked her lips unconsciously and swallowed when their gazes crossed.

He cut the boards as she measured, and she grew easier with the task as they went, zipping out the tape measure and drawing the cut line with efficiency and confidence.

The last board, he took from her, then said, "Come cut it!"

"Oh, I couldn't," she protested. "It's so…loud. I'd cut off a finger or something."

"It's perfectly safe," Travis assured her. He showed her the cutting guard that came down to cover the blade, and put his hands over hers to show her where to safely hold the board and how to snug it up against the cutting guide.

He put her hands on the trigger and let her rev the blade up, letting her experience how quickly it would brake when she let go and what it would sound like, then stepped back. "Go for it!"

Jenny bit her lip, scrunched her whole face in concentration, and cut the board with one smooth, slow motion.

"Oh my gosh," she squeaked, when she had released the trigger and returned the chop saw to its upright position. "That was the most exciting thing I've ever done!"

Travis had to grin at her enthusiasm. He refrained from the obvious comment that her life must not be all that exciting.

She helped him carry the board to the bare deck joists and hold it in place while he screwed it into place. "Here," he said, passing her the tool.

She took it gingerly, then stared when he didn't make a move to take it back. "Wait, you want me to do this part?

Oh, no, I'm no good at this kind of thing. I tried using a power drill once and couldn't even get one screw in. I chipped the drywall and still couldn't hang up my picture." She shook her head vehemently.

"Let me introduce you to the joy that is the impact driver," Travis said, covering her hands on the tool reassuringly. He showed her how to hold it, and what to do with the hose that snaked away from it to the air compressor. The screws had special heads that fit into a closed bit, and Travis demonstrated how to make sure the screws wouldn't wobble as they were driven in.

Then he moved back and let Jenny try her own. At first she was ginger with the screw, then bore down with more strength, and the screw shrieked into the lumber and left a little dimple in the board.

"Wow!" Jenny exclaimed, giving Travis a sunny smile. "That was so easy!"

Travis laughed with her. "My grandmother always said that no woman needs a man if she has the right tools."

Jenny look admiringly at the impact driver. "This is definitely the right tool," she said, nodding.

"My grandmother was a dirty old woman, and I think she was talking about something else entirely," Travis told her with a grin. "But it's still very true."

Jenny laughed, and it was the first time that Travis had seen her truly relaxed. "Can I do it again?"

He showed her how to adjust the resistance so that the screws went in just the right amount, then let her screw in the rest of the board. They brought the next piece, aligning it with spacers. He screwed in the first two, then let her go wild with the driver while he brought the next board over.

With two sets of hands, the work went very quickly,

and in no time at all, they were screwing the railing back onto the new deck.

"I've never made anything before," Jenny said, standing back to admire their work. "What a feeling!"

"There's nothing like it," Travis said, but he wasn't looking at the deck.

She looked up to catch his gaze. "There really isn't," she agreed.

Travis didn't stop to ask permission this time, taking the invitation in her eyes as consent. He gathered her into his arms and kissed her with all the passion in his heart.

16

*J*enny had read plenty of romance novels. She knew all the best descriptions for kisses and things more intimate. She was guilty of lingering over scenes of tenderness and the sweet nothings that the heroes would murmur as they caressed their lovers.

But romance writers, she realized in that moment, knew nothing.

It wasn't weak knees and gentle words. It was raw and animal, an utterly primal power that made every nerve ending in her body come alive with the touch of his lips on hers. It was need and strength, in the feel of his sweat-beaded muscles under her fingers. For a moment, she wished she still had claws, because she wanted to sink into that flesh and claim him as her own.

His fingers were impossibly strong, pulling at her shoulders, kneading at her waist, and Jenny wondered if she would have bruises that wouldn't show on her deep brown skin. She wanted bruises. She wanted marks of their lovemaking, and when Travis groaned and tried to gentle his hands, she pressed harder into him.

"The deck," she hissed near his ear. "I want to make love on the deck we built."

Her breath left her lungs as Travis lifted her effortlessly and carried her onto the new deck, laying her sensibly in the only bit of shade. The morning had gotten unexpectedly hot, and already, her entire body was moist with sweat.

It made every touch electric, and as wet as her body was, between her legs was a wetter place still. Travis peeled off her soaking underwear, and pulled her dress off over her head in one musical move. He was shucking off his own clothing with an eagerness that made him almost clumsy, and Jenny drank in the sight of him.

His cock sprang out eagerly, rigid and thick. Gold-skinned muscles gleamed with dappled sunlight and perspiration, a fascinating rippling effect that made Jenny flex her hands helplessly as she waited.

She did have long to wait, then he was straddling her, spreading her legs and thrusting into her without any of the preambles of the night before.

Their previous encounter had been lovemaking, this was just fucking, and Jenny loved every moment of it. She arched up to him, crying out and clawing at the boards they had so recently screwed in. He set a brutal, desperate pace to his thrusts, growling near her ear as she panted and met every stroke.

She came like an explosion, feeling the release ripple through her entire body right to her toes. Travis slowed his motions to let the decrescendo of her orgasm last longer, then slipped entirely out of her, gritting his teeth as he paused to delay his own release and prolong their fun. Jenny gave a cry of loss as he left her, but when he had recovered his control and made a motion to resume where they had left off, she sat up and pushed him back down.

She straddled him authoritatively, holding down his thick arms as if she had any chance of keeping him in place, and he grinned at her in delight and desire.

She teased him for a long moment, just touching the end of his quivering penis with her outer folds, letting him get only the head into her places of pleasure before retreating again. She leaned over to kiss his neck, sliding teeth over his collarbone and shoulders, licking, and letting her breasts, sensitive nipples fully erect, slide over his sweat-slick chest.

He groaned and thrust his hips at her, but let her continue to hold him down, though the muscles bunched up several times as if he wished to break free.

Then, finally, she buried him into her, letting his member fill her entirely, and then held herself there. The noise he made was half delight and half agony of desire, and he bucked against her. She locked around him, keeping him from retreating for a full stroke, and kept her motions to small, torturous gyrations.

She wasn't sure who finally gave in, whether she began the rhythmic strokes, in and out, or if he made it happen. His hands were on her hips, and she wasn't sure when she'd let go of his arms and put her hands on his shoulders; her world was reduced to the friction and pressure and throb of the pleasure he was raising inexorably in her.

When she came again, he did as well, and Jenny could feel the pulse of his release deep within her as all of his muscles turned to rock beneath her hands and her world reduced to light and completion.

When she could remember herself again, she was sprawled on top of Travis, both of them slick with sweat and other fluids, breath heavy in each others ears.

She felt satisfied. From the lobes of her ears to the heels of her feet, she was exactly where she wanted to be, her whole body feeling comfortably used.

"I think I have a splinter in my ass," Travis told her, and the laughter came through his chest into Jenny's ears and infected her until she couldn't do anything but giggle helplessly, clasp her sides, and gasp for breath.

"Let's go take a shower," Jenny suggested, sitting up at last.

"We should have the staff house to ourselves at this time of day," Travis said, rising to his feet and helping her up.

Jenny picked up her dress and looked down at her body. "I don't really want to put this on," she said.

Travis picked up his own clothing, but made no move to put any of it on. "Lucky you, the resort is clothing optional."

Otter cheered in her head.

Jenny's reluctance must have shown on her face, and Travis assured her, "I'll take you around the back way. We probably won't meet anyone."

Jenny stood up straight. "Alright, then," she said, putting her hand in the crook of his elbow that he offered. "Let's go get cleaned up."

17

"...*A*nd then we gave the new decking a good load test," Travis said with a grin that felt like it was going to split his face.

Tex clapped him cheerfully on the shoulder. "Good for you!" he cheered.

"Dooooooom," was Breck's contribution.

"Details, man!" Bastian demanded.

But just then, Jenny appeared at the door to the kitchen, looking gorgeous and freshly showered. Breck and Bastian greeted her politely and excused themselves.

"Lunch rush is about to start," Breck explained. "As much of a rush as eight guests can be!"

"Going to grab food from the buffet and head to the pool," Bastian said with a wave.

The front door clicked shut behind them, but the open windows made their parting conversation carry clearly: "Damn, I need some of that mate action."

"Are you an idiot, man? Flex your muscles at one of the guests and get a room key or three, but don't ever wish for a mate."

"Good moooorning," Laura sang as she and Tex came down the stairs behind Jenny, propelling her into the kitchen.

Travis finally stopped staring and stepped forward to give Jenny a quick, shy kiss on the cheek once she was in reach, hyper-aware of her twin sister and her mate at the kitchen bar behind him. Jenny grinned as foolishly at him as he knew she was at her.

"After lunch, I was going to go try to help Scarlet with that contract she was asking about," she said, accepting the plate Travis had already prepared and sitting with him at the kitchen bar. "I was able to read some of those magazines that I know you guys only have around for the articles, so I think I can probably make some sense out of Scarlet's contract now."

"Fantastic," Travis said.

"You never doubted for a moment, did you," Jenny said in wonder.

"Not for a second," Travis could say in all honesty.

"That makes one of us." Jenny was even beautiful when she ate, with graceful fingers, and a mesmerizing mouth. Travis realized he was staring and had to concentrate on eating his own food, glancing up to see that Jenny was watching him as avidly as he'd been watching her.

Their exchange of gazes did not go unnoticed.

"Oh, aren't they adorable," Laura said sweetly to Tex.

"Like a southern lemonade," he agreed. "New mates, you know. Can't keep their eyes off each other."

"You speak from such a position of superiority," Travis said dryly. "Being a whole week ahead of us at this."

"You know, I'm older than you by six minutes," Jenny reminded her.

"But not wiser," Laura said mockingly.

Travis thought it sounded like an exchange they'd had many times.

Jenny took her plate to the trash and brushed off the crumbs before putting her dishes in the dishwasher.

"I've got a bathroom to re-tile," Travis said, following suit.

"Tiling sounds really complicated," Jenny admitted, as they put their shoes on at the front door.

"It's pretty straight-forward," Travis said modestly. "I could show you how to do it."

Jenny's eyes danced with amusement. "I'll come by after I'm done with Scarlet, and we can test the final product."

"Get a room!" Laura laughed at them from the kitchen.

"Yes, ma'am!" Tex loudly and deliberately misunderstood her, and there was a playful shriek and the smack of a loud kiss.

Travis took Jenny's hand as they left the house, and it was incredibly delightful just to have to her hand in his, fingers entwined. He was reluctant to let her go when their paths diverged, and he drew her in for a long, lingering kiss.

"I'm looking forward to seeing you later," he said, when he finally released her lips.

"Me, too," she said breathlessly back.

He stole one final kiss, then turned his back decisively and marched away down the path, glancing over his shoulder to find that Jenny was walking backwards so she could smile after him. She gave him two thumbs up and mouthed "Great ass!" before turning and scampering up the steps towards the top of the resort.

18

*J*enny was smiling and watching her feet as she wandered up the steps and steep paths towards the place where Scarlet's office perched at the top of the resort.

The building was empty.

Jenny waited a short while in the green, shady court-yard, wandering between the plants and reading the little tags that were in with each one. She fingered one of the flowers, but remembered Travis' warning about picking anything, and left it in peace.

After a while, she wandered back down to the bar deck, where Tex was polishing each of the bottles to a sparkling luster. Jenny walked to the railing to look below.

Magnolia waved at her from one of the deck chairs, and she waved back with a shy smile. The only other person on the deck was a tattooed man built like a small tank, who looked up over his sunglasses when Magnolia waved.

"Where's Laura?" she asked, returning to the bar and sitting on one of the bar stools. She'd rather go find Travis, but was hesitant to interrupt his work more than she already had. Despite his assurances, she suspected that laying tile was a tad more complicated than she was up for and knew she'd only slow him down. She waved off Tex's offer for a drink; she didn't want to freeload at the resort any more than she had to.

"Lydia is taking some time off, because the incoming storm has scared some of the guests off, so Laura offered to help out in the spa," Tex said. He showed her on the brochure where the spa was, circling it with a pen.

"Thanks," Jenny said, and she slipped off the stool to find her sister. She paused and turned back around. "Thanks for... being great for my sister."

Tex gave her a soft, crooked smile. "She's everything to me," he admitted without shame.

"I can tell," Jenny said thoughtfully. "And she adores you, too."

"Much like you and Travis," Tex said gently.

Jenny gazed back at him. She and Travis hadn't said anything about love, but she wondered if he felt it as deeply as she did. Tex seemed to accept it as foregone, but was it, really?

"Thanks again," Jenny said, taking the brochure that Tex had marked up.

She breathed deeply, wondering if she was imagining the strange feeling of pressure and rain in the air. It was sweltering hot and clear, and the path to the spa was steep, like most of the walkways in the resort, but a stiff breeze had sprung up.

Footsteps crunching swiftly in the gravel behind her made her turn curiously and find the hulking man from the pool deck following her. He didn't look like a good candidate for the spa, but they did animal grooming as well. Maybe he was going to get a good brushing. Jenny nodded politely and turned back to the path in front of her, scooting over so that he could pass her, as he seemed to be in a hurry.

Her otter screamed a warning at her too late for her to dodge the crushing blow that came from one of his large fists, and Jenny's world went to blackness.

19

*T*ravis was kneeling in the work area, splattered to the elbows in grout and cutting one of the tricky corner pieces when Lynx yowled inside him, all claws and panic.

He dropped the tile, not even caring that it broke, and leaped to his feet.

Lynx couldn't lead him, only knew that something was wrong, that his mate was in trouble, that they had to do *something*. So Travis went to the bar, and he came in the back entrance just as Laura came sprinting from the side entrance. Not for a moment did he think she was Jenny.

"Something is wrong," he said, fighting down Lynx's blind panic.

"Something is very wrong," Laura agreed, eyes wild.

Tex put his guitar down. "What is it?" he asked, looking from one to the other in growing alarm.

"Jenny, she's gone." Laura tapped the side of her head.

"She's hurt," Travis added. Lynx snarled and Travis could feel him pacing anxiously.

Tex came out from around the bar. "I told her you

were at the spa, love," he told Laura, reaching out for her hand. "Ten minutes ago, maybe fifteen."

"I didn't see her there," Laura insisted. "I just came from there, I would have seen her!"

Travis, finally with a direction to go, loped for the path to the spa, every sense alert for some clue to what had happened, and where his mate was. Laura and Tex were close on his heels.

"Hold up!" Tex said, coming to a stop behind him.

Travis turned to see Tex standing up with a discarded brochure that Travis had ignored, blown up into the hedge. The spa was circled in pen. "This is the brochure I gave Jenny."

Laura gave a little moan of worry and Tex put an arm around her. "We'll find her," he promised.

"Can you smell her?" Travis demanded. Lynx had hearing so keen he could tell when an engine was the smallest bit out of alignment, but he couldn't smell a cigar a meter away. Tex, on the other hand, had a bear's better-than-bloodhound nose.

Tex gave a sniff, walking in a circle around the area where he'd found the brochure. Finally, he shrugged and shook his head. "Guests, staff, Laura... I can't smell Jenny specifically, or tell where she is."

Travis snarled and balled helpless hands at his side. "Someone *took* her," he insisted.

The distant sound of the resort van coughing into life was clear to Travis' keen hearing. "And with no boat, there's only one way off this island!"

Travis bolted for the resort entrance.

20

*J*enny woke when the van went around a hairpin curve and she slid into the side of the vehicle.

"Ow," she said out loud before she could stop herself.

"Dammit," a rough voice said. She realized after a moment that it wasn't addressed at her.

"No, I told you, I'm gonna need that plane now. I don't care if there's a storm incoming. This place is crawling with shifters. The lifeguard is a dragon, did you know that? Yeah. They're gonna come looking for her, I haven't got that kind of time."

There was a pause in the conversation and Jenny was able to lever herself up and peer over the back of the second seat back. The driver was the gorilla from the pool deck, wearing clothing now, and the throbbing in Jenny's head suggested that it was his fist that had caused her unconsciousness. Her hands were tied together, and just as she was considering whether she could shift her way out of the knots and escape, she met his eyes in the rear view mirror.

"Shit," he said. "And fuck you, too," he added as an afterthought into the phone. "It better be there when we get there. That was the agreement." He hung it up as vehemently as he could with a tiny button on a tiny box that was dwarfed by his large hand.

"Don't try shifting," he warned Jenny. "I've drugged you with some fancy shit that should prevent you from shifting into a wolf or any other magic crap. Man, is your boss pissed at you right now."

Jenny was trying to wrap her head around why anyone at the firm would be this angry with her when the specific words from his statement sunk in. A wolf. They thought she was a wolf shifter like Laura. No, they thought she *was* Laura. This pleasant mountain of a man must have been sent by the mob that her twin sister had worked for.

Was he telling the truth about shifting?

Jenny reached for the otter within her, and was alarmed to find silence. She reached for Laura then, trying to use their odd twin bond to make some kind of meaningful contact. Silence met her again. Though her head throbbed, Jenny didn't think it was just a concussion. The mating bond... that was stronger than either of those things, wasn't it?

Travis...

Jenny scrunched her eyes together against the pain that bloomed behind her eyes at the effort.

"I'm not Laura," she said.

"Sure you're not," the man laughed gruffly. His voice went mockingly high. "You've got the wrong guy, mister! I swear!"

"I have a twin sister," Jenny said, offended.

"Oh, that's a good one," the man said flatly. "I've never heard that one before." His flat tone suggested otherwise.

The road they were traveling was full of tight corners

and steep grades. Jenny found that her feet had also been tied, and it was a challenge to remain upright without being able to spread her limbs. She wedged herself against the window, and glared at the man in the rear view mirror.

"What are you going to do with me?" she asked.

"I'm just the collector," he said. "I deliver you to your boss in LA and get paid. Blacksmith said in one piece if possible, but he wasn't too picky. Guess he's not so happy that half his crew got nabbed by the pigs a few days back."

His phone rang then, and he nearly missed a curve answering it. "Wrench," he said sharply.

It took Jenny a moment to realize he meant it as his name.

He glanced back at her, listening to the phone intensely. He swapped ears, navigating another corner and a series of epic potholes. "I know," he said, clearly trying to keep his voice down. "I'm on a good job right now, I'll have the money real soon."

Jenny's otter senses weren't all gone; she could hear him without effort, even over the sounds of the van and the rising wind outside. The jungle was whipping alarmingly, and in the few places they drove through clear areas, she could see Wrench struggling to control the van against the wind.

"No, it's a sure thing. You can sign her up for the class, I'll make sure it gets paid."

Jenny could almost hear the voice at the other end, but not quite.

"Yeah," Wrench said ambiguously. It was night and day how different his voice was on this conversation compared to the last. "Can I talk to her?"

If his voice had been less gruff with this conversation, it was now an order of magnitude more gentle, and as quiet as Wrench could manage. "Hey, kitten!"

The chatter at the other end was even clearer, high-pitched and eager. Jenny could make out the words ballet, friends, music, and dancing. She watched Wrench in the mirror, re-evaluating him as he conversed with the girl at the other end of the phone. Even his face softened, and when he took off his sunglasses because the sky was growing dark, his eyes looked gentle.

Was this Stockholm syndrome? Jenny wondered. It wasn't that she didn't still want to kick the man in the knees, but it was hard to hate someone who would buy ballet lessons for a little girl. Even if it was with dirty kidnapping money.

"I gotta go, kitten," Wrench said at last, as they broke out of the jungle at the end of the little airstrip. Barely audible, he added, "Love you," before hanging up and glaring suspiciously at Jenny in the mirror.

Jenny pretended that she hadn't heard a word, and wondered if she'd imagined the gentleness.

Wrench parked the van at the end of the runway, and cursed when he opened his door and the wind blew it shut before he could get out.

Jenny considered struggling when Wrench came around the van to pull her out, but she knew at once that it would be futile and settled for stomping on his foot as he set her down. She tried again to shift to her otter shape, and the wave of dizziness that came with the effort made her almost fall over.

But she could tell that whatever it was she'd been given was weakening. Her otter was *there* again, growling and gnashing sharp teeth in frustration. Jenny played up her dizziness and slumped into Wrench.

Wrench cut the cords at her ankles, and hauled her to her feet. Jenny knew she had no chance of outrunning him in this form; she had enough trouble standing upright against the whipping wind.

Wrench's phone rang and he answered it with a growl of his name, turning away from the wind and repeating it louder when it wasn't heard the first time.

"He's nuts to try it," he shouted. "But we're waiting."

He hung up, and pulled Jenny into the dubious shelter behind the van.

Jenny looked at the way the trees were bending in the gusts. "You might want to make sure they know what to do with your money when you die in a fiery plane crash. Wouldn't want your kitten to default on her ballet lessons."

She was rewarded with Wrench's alarmed, embarrassed look. "You've got better ears than I thought," he snarled, not amused. "I'll be glad to hand you off."

The rumble of the approaching airplane was hard even for Jenny to hear over the wind, which was now roaring, crosswise to the runway. She pointed her bound hands in that direction. "Well, here it comes now."

Wrench looked, and they both watched in horror as the little plane was caught in a gust, twisted sideways and overcorrected, spitting back out over the ocean to crash into the waves offshore.

21

*T*ravis skidded to a stop at the top of the resort.

The van was long gone, down the winding jungle road that led to the airfield on the other side of the island.

He howled in rage, and Tex and Laura, panting, came up behind him.

"I thought that Costa Rica didn't get hurricanes," Tex said, staring at the sky and holding onto his hat. There were thick dark clouds gathering north of the island, and the wind was beginning to pick up with a vengeance.

"This isn't a hurricane," Breck said, coming out of the office. "Have you seen Scarlet? Did she take the van?" He looked from one to the other, picking up on the urgency of the situation. "What's going on?"

"We don't know who took the van," Tex said.

"But whoever it is, they've got Jenny," Travis told him, gnashing his teeth.

"I can't feel her," Laura said in anguish. "Not... not quite like before, it's a little different. Like there's cotton between us."

"Yes," Travis said, glad for her words to put what he was feeling into context. "That's exactly what it's like."

Breck looked from one to the other in growing alarm. "Kidnapped? Who would kidnap her?"

"Fred?" Tex suggested.

"He's still in prison," Laura said, shaking her head. "This feels more like the cartel's M.O."

"The cartel?" Breck asked in disbelief.

"It's a long story," Laura said.

"There was a last-minute guest who arrived yesterday who looks the part," Breck suggested. "Southern Californian for sure, lots of scars and tattoos."

"Mr. Muscles with the suitcases of lead," Tex said, snapping his fingers.

"Why are we not going after them already?" Travis asked, snarling.

"We couldn't catch them now," Tex cautioned. "They're halfway to the airstrip, and none of us are distance runners in either form."

"Who would send a plane in this weather?" Breck scoffed. "The regular charter got canceled. Anyway, take the Jeep."

The others looked at him with sudden hope. "It's running?"

"A little rough," Breck said with false modesty. "I've still got to rebuild the carburetor one of these days..."

Travis was already pushing past him to where it was parked. "I'll drive," he said.

22

---

*T*he wings of the plane tore off as if they'd been made of paper when it hit the ocean. It made a terrible ripping sound even louder than the roaring wind, and the fuselage sank with a rush of bubbles and screaming metal.

Jenny and Wrench watched in astonishment.

"We should see if anyone survived," she said, finally. "They might need help."

Wrench squinted at her. "You do realize that they were here to drag you back to the cartel."

Jenny glared back at him. "I'm not saying that they aren't terrible people, but they are still *people*. Drowning is a horrible way to go, and I should know it."

Wrench tried to stare her down. "It's not like you can shift yet," he said.

Jenny closed her eyes and reached down inside of her. Her otter wriggled to greet her, eager to breach the prison she'd been trapped in.

If she concentrated… just like so… she could almost feel the barrier keeping them apart. And if she could just burn it away, she could shift again, and sense Laura again, and reach Travis. Travis. She longed for his touch, his comfort. Even just knowing that he was there.

Something Gizelle had said to her bubbled out of her memory. Much of what she said was rambling and disjointed, and Jenny had learned to filter out some of the more absurd statements, but something the gazelle shifter had said about power stuck with her.

"There is power below you, if you can reach it," Gizelle had told her. "Sunlit caverns with no sky." She'd been talking about the power required for shifting, but Jenny had to wonder.

The sky above them now was dark and weirdly hard to see, even to Jenny's enhanced otter sight, and Jenny wondered if she imagined the power that crackled between sky and island. They felt... connected, as if the island itself had drawn the storm to it.

Jenny reached, and she wasn't sure if she was reaching above her to the storm, or below her to the depths of the island, only knew that she had to shift, and that she needed to break her otter out of her trap, and that the means were here, within her reach.

Power answered her, bright and clear and terrifying in its intensity, and otter sprang from her in the smoothest shift that Jenny had yet managed.

The restraints fell away from her small paws and Jenny was scampering away from Wrench as he cursed and grabbed for her.

She could escape, she realized, exactly as she realized with a wave of relief that Travis and Laura were back in her head with her, along with her otter self. All she had to do was get away from Wrench and hide.

Even as she thought it, she knew she couldn't turn her back to any survivors that might be out in the plane. She had the ability to lead them safely back to shore, and she had to try.

Jenny turned back to Wrench, to find a pitch black panther standing in a pile of shredded clothing. Perhaps getting free would not have been as easy as she'd first thought.

But he didn't pounce, and after a long moment of mutual consideration, Jenny turned her back on him and ran for the ocean, diving in without hesitation.

23

"*J*enny!" Travis said, nearly losing control of the Jeep around one of the hairpin curves.

"What the hell?" Breck yelled, clutching at the seat and glove box handles.

"She's okay!" Laura shouted with tremendous relief from the seat behind them where she was sitting with Tex.

"What was that?" Travis asked, twisting to look back at her.

"The road!" Breck hollered. "Please watch the road!"

"I have no idea," Laura said, looking as shaken as he felt.

It had felt as if their bond had been lit on fire, all the cotton burned away in a fiery blast.

Jenny, Travis thought fiercely, desperately.

And clear as a summer day, her voice came to him.

Travis! I'm alright!

Where are you? He asked, relief in every cell of his body.

The answer was wry amusement and a sense that it was complicated. *In the ocean. Rescuing the people who tried to kidnap me.*

Travis laughed out loud. Of course she was.

"She's free," he told the others. "But we need to get to the airstrip."

"On, James," mocked Breck, and Travis shifted gears as he drove around another tight corner, fighting the Jeep against the wind that was driving hard out the low, dark sky.

24

*J*enny reached the wreckage in no time, swimming mostly underwater. She scanned the water for any sign of human survivors, diving under the surface to find any sunken bodies. She found that her otter had a strange vibration sense, and she listened for any motions in the water, someone swimming or struggling.

The water rippled with the force of the wind over top of it, but was quiet further down. The song of the ocean was still peaceful here, water buffering the power of the storm, and dampening the strange energy of the island. There were fish, going about their fishy business, and she almost went swimming after them before her human self reminded her firmly about why they were here.

It occurred to her again that she had no compulsion to return to the shore where Wrench waited. All she had to do was swim away, safe in her otter form from whatever the storm threw at her.

But that wouldn't keep Wrench from trying again, and perhaps getting Laura for real next time.

Jenny bobbed to the surface, looking for anyone clinging to floating debris. She nosed through pieces of fuselage, and parts of seats. Bits of unidentifiable plastic cluttered the surface, confusing her otter senses. Finally, she gave up, and she was just debating her return to the shore again when she found a floating briefcase.

While she didn't see anything special about it at first, her human gave a crow of triumph at spotting it, convinced that it had that spy movie ransom suitcase look. She swam over and wrapped her small forearms around it, then tugged herself onto her back to drag it to the beach.

Loaded thusly, her return trip was much harder and lengthier than her trip out, but Jenny doggedly continued, practicing her negotiation with Wrench in her head. He could have the briefcase, and would leave Jenny and Laura alone forever. Maybe he could convince the cartel that her sister had died when he tried to bring her in.

Just as the ocean floor rose beneath her to become the beach and the water turned to surf, she heard the comforting voice of her mate in her head. *Jenny! We're here!*

Before she could answer, there was a predator's shriek of rage from above, and Jenny was struck with outstretched talons, losing her grip on the suitcase as she was lifted into the air by something with wide, sweeping wings.

---

25

*T*ravis would never have driven so fast, on roads so terrible, for any other reason.

But his mate needed him, and he wasn't going to risk being too late to the scene.

When they finally broke out of the jungle onto the airstrip, he didn't even hesitate before gunning directly at the huge, naked man with tattoos and scars who was standing with his back to them on the far side of the field. He knew without a shadow of doubt that this was the man who had stolen his mate, and Travis had no qualms about running him down on the spot.

Breck, Tex, and Laura all yelled, and Travis wasn't sure if they were warning the man, trying to stop him, giving voice to the warcry in his own thoughts, or just screaming. At the last moment, the man leaped out of the way in a dark, shifting blur as the Jeep smashed through the place he was standing, and jostled down the bank of the narrow beach to stick fast into a pile of driftwood.

They spilled out of the Jeep and faced down the panther that glared at them from the bank.

Breck, who had already shed his clothing with the swiftness of consistent practice, shifted into a spotted leopard. Travis heard Tex and Laura growl beside him, still human, but flexing their hands.

The panther shimmered and stood up as a man again, hands spread. "I haven't got her," he said, not bothering to deny that he had once.

"Where is she?" Travis demanded.

The man pointed, out at the surf, where a tiny dark form was struggling out of the water, dragging a piece of debris. Further out, large pieces of smoking wreckage indicated that something had just crashed into the ocean.

Jenny, Travis thought at her. *We're here!*

Just then, an eagle shrieked and plummeted down from the stormy sky, talons outstretched, and plucked Jenny from the water.

Travis gave a cry that matched that of the predator bird and was hurling down the beach without thinking about it. He could feel Jenny's pain and shock as the talons gripped her mercilessly and hauled her into the air.

"Jenny!" Laura shrieked behind him.

The eagle struggled against the wind, nearly falling back into the surf before it gained enough lift to land with Jenny's limp form onto a tall tangle of driftwood. He put his beak around Jenny's throat and lifted her that way, flaring his wings in clear threat; he could easily break her neck.

Travis drew to a stop at the base of the driftwood, a snarling bear and whining wolf at one side and Breck's leopard at the other. "Let her go!" Only the need for human speech kept him from shifting.

"Hey now!" the man from the resort bellowed, muscling his way fearlessly between Travis and the bear. "That's not the right woman! We're after a wolf shifter!"

The eagle shrugged into a human form, deftly transferring his hold from beak to big hands. Jenny's otter neck was clearly no safer in one than the other — a single motion would break it easily. Jenny remained limp and unresisting, though Travis could feel her coiled energy through their bond.

"Let her go," Laura yelled, shifting into her human form and standing tall and proud despite her nudity. "He's right. I'm the one you want."

Tex shifted as well. "Laura…" he growled, almost lost against the wind.

"Boss won't care which of you he gets," the eagle shifter shrugged, with a cruel smile. "You've caused a lot of trouble in the organization, and either way, you'll pay for it."

The guest from Shifting Sands made a noise of protest that Travis wouldn't have heard if he hadn't been standing so close, then hollered, "You can't nab the wrong woman. She swam out there to try to save you."

The eagle shifter didn't look impressed. "Your vacation make you soft, Wrench? The boss wants revenge. Doesn't much matter how he gets it."

"I got a code," Wrench returned stubbornly.

"I got a code!" The eagle mocked in a falsetto. Then he returned to his usual voice. "Well, I got a job to finish."

"Let's make a call," Wrench suggested, as the eagle shifter raised his hand to make show of wringing Jenny's neck. "See what Blacksmith says direct."

Travis was done waiting for something else to happen. He bunched his muscles, preparing to shift.

Travis, be ready, warned Jenny, and Travis paused.

Wrench had all of the man's attention. "Make a call?" he taunted. "What are you in kindergarten calling your Mommy?"

Now! Jenny cried, and she twisted in the eagle shifter's hands and sank sharp teeth into the tender webbing of his thumb.

26

*J*enny was not surprised when the eagle shifter dropped her and then missed at grabbing her again. His hands scrambled for her lithe, flexible otter body as she twisted and kicked away with clawed feet. While she struggled, she caught sight of Travis out of the corner of her eye, clothing shedding from him as he shifted, and leaped impossibly high into the air as a lynx to land on the driftwood beside her captor.

Jenny landed on her side with a thump in the sand that left her dazed, and scrambled to her feet, shifting back to human as she went.

Naked man versus enraged lynx was no match, but eagle was better suited for the battle.

Powerful wings battered at Travis, and sharp, wicked talons tore into his thick-furred shoulder.

Jenny bit back her cry of alarm, not wanting to be a fatal distraction at an inopportune point.

Travis shredded in return, using long, curved claws on powerful paws, sinking snarling teeth into the eagle's wing.

The eagle gave a cry of agony and rage, and snapped

his strong, sharp beak at Travis, who was too fast for the assault.

Their battle sent them tumbling off the driftwood, and Jenny might have been knocked by one of the eagle's massive wings if Laura hadn't pulled her back out of the way.

Then there was a second big cat in the fray, and a massive brown bear waded in, snarling ferociously.

Jenny and Laura held each other and watched in alarm as claws and teeth flashed and feathers flew in the howling wind.

Knowing he was outnumbered, the eagle tried to shake them off and escape into the sky, but between the bleeding teeth marks in his wing and the wild, erratic wind, he was easily dragged back to the earth.

He was quickly overwhelmed, and shifted back to his human form with Travis' teeth at his throat.

"Mercy!" The shifter begged pathetically.

Travis, still a lynx, remained at his throat, growling, but didn't close his grip. The others backed away, but not far.

"You can't kill a man who's begging," the mobster whined.

Wrench had stayed back from the battle, but stepped forward now. "I thought you didn't have a code," he said scornfully.

Travis shifted back into human at last, and Jenny had to hold herself back from running to him. Blood oozed down his shoulder.

"Well, you're just lucky I do," he said, standing up and backing away.

Just then, the skies opened up and it began to pour.

27

*I*t took all of Travis' self-control to back away from his prey, helpless and bloody in the wet sand now.

But he was aware of Jenny, behind him, and was so glad and relieved that she was unharmed that the fate of the eagle shifter swiftly became unimportant to him.

When Breck and Tex moved forward to secure the now-sodden shifter, he could finally turn away, and Jenny ran into his arms.

She was soaking wet, her sundress plastered to every gorgeous curve. Travis gathered her up in his arms, giving a little gasp as his shoulder reminded him that it had recently been pierced by eagle talons. It wasn't anything a few shifts and a couple of hours of healing wouldn't fix, but it was still bleeding sluggishly and Jenny exclaimed over it in concern when he set her back down on her feet.

It was a subdued party that returned to the Jeep, scavenging the parts of their clothing that they could. Tex and Travis, with the help of Wrench, were able to push the

Jeep back out of the driftwood tangle that Travis had driven it into.

"Sorry I tried to run you down," Travis said cautiously to the big man.

"Sorry I tried to kidnap your girlfriend," Wrench replied in the same grave tone.

The eagle shifter was bound at the wrists using a roll of duct tape from the Jeep toolbox, and Wrench was left free.

"You aren't planning to try anything on the real Laura, are you?" Tex's tone might have been taken as teasing, but the way he bared his teeth at Wrench was serious. He was still holding the duct tape.

Wrench looked conflicted, then shook his head. "I ain't usually sent after people that don't deserve it," he said with a shrug of his shoulders. "But this time... I'm not gonna turn you over."

"What are you going to tell them?" Laura asked.

Wrench shrugged. "Failure ain't taken lightly by these guys, you should know."

"Oh!" Jenny said suddenly, and she turned and scampered down the beach.

Travis watched her go, thinking she looked sexier than ever and wishing that no one else was around. He wanted to lay her down in the sand and make love to her in the pouring rain, never mind his bleeding shoulder or the storm that was still crashing around them.

The heaviness of the driving rain nearly made her disappear as she waded into the heavy surf and she returned after a long moment, triumphantly carrying a briefcase.

She handed it to Wrench.

"That will probably pay for some dancing classes," she said mysteriously.

Wrench looked like he might cry, an odd look for a

naked, hulking man covered in scars and tattoos. He cracked it open, and several American dollar bills fluttered out in a gust of wind before he could snap it shut.

"Or," Jenny continued, "You could turn it over as evidence against them and go the legal route and bear witness against your boss. You could get out of the business for good."

Wrench stared at her.

"I can't promise you wouldn't do time," she said. "But being cooperative would be very helpful to your cause, and I can recommend a good criminal lawyer."

"Doin' time again don't scare me," Wrench grumbled, scowling ferociously down at her. "But that don't fix the question of what I do afterwards. I like the idea of clean work, but no one good hires cons."

"Scarlet might," Travis suggested.

Tex and Breck looked at him, and Breck nodded. "She might," he agreed with a shrug. "Graham's done time."

"For what?" Tex asked in surprise.

"Murder," Breck said merrily.

"Murder?" exclaimed Jenny. "I didn't know that."

"Makes you reconsider having sex in the flower beds, doesn't it," Tex laughed

"Nah," Travis said, with a sideways glance at Jenny, who looked embarrassed, but rolled her eyes at him good-naturedly.

"Not for a minute," Breck added with a satisfied look.

"I'm soaking," Laura said firmly. "Let's go home."

"I'm driving the van back," Breck announced. "Travis almost killed us driving here, and it wasn't even raining then." He was fully dressed again, having stripped his clothing sensibly before shifting. Tex's clothing was rather worse for the wear; his staff uniform was equal parts shredded and soaking. Travis' clothing was in better shape, his lynx being smaller in size, but still badly ripped.

Laura's dress would be fine with small repairs, and Jenny, Travis realized with some surprise, had never lost her dress.

Part of him was selfishly disappointed.

*B*y the time they arrived at the resort, the worst of the storm had blown over.

There were several downed trees along the way, or at least big parts of them, and Jenny didn't mind watching Travis haul the ones they couldn't drive over out of the way with Wrench and Tex, marveling at his strength.

The resort itself was scattered with broken tree limbs and shredded flowers.

"I am going to hide from Graham for a week," Breck said, surveying the damage.

"We're going to have to repair several of the roofs," Travis said thoughtfully, looking down over the cottages. "I could use your help on that, Wrench."

Jenny thought Wrench looked touched. "I got no fear of heights," he rumbled. "But you'd have to teach me how."

"He's a very good teacher," Jenny assured him.

The rain had reduced to a faint drizzle, and the wind was almost nothing now.

Scarlet met them at the empty bar, looking a little wild-eyed, and as disheveled as Jenny had ever seen her.

"I trust you have an interesting story to share regarding the reason all of my primary staff have been missing for several hours," she said, looking at the trussed up eagle shifter with narrow eyes.

He responded with a string of expletives that made Tex tsk disapprovingly and slap a piece of duct tape over his mouth.

"We've got another charming character for the civil guard to pick up," Breck told Scarlet. "And some more paperwork for our friend Tony."

Wrench, recognizing her authority, handed her the briefcase, a little reluctantly.

"I'm willing to bear witness against the cartel what hired me," he said gruffly. "And I'd take a job, if you had one."

Scarlet looked at the briefcase distastefully, but took it. "I don't run a charity," she said crossly.

"I ain't afraid of hard work," Wrench assured her. "And I'm not too good to get dirty."

"We'll see," Scarlet said, her chilly voice without promise. "Let's put this guy in the usual place," she gestured at the eagle shifter, who was seething and working his mouth behind the duct tape. "Breck, catch me up on the details, and I'll call Tony." Her low heels clicked away across the wet tile decisively. "Have you seen Bastian?"

Breck poked the eagle shifter and marched him after her. "Not since this morning."

"Jenny!" Gizelle's hair was more wild than ever, and she looked as if she'd spent the storm cavorting in a field.

It occurred to Jenny that she might have done just that.

Gizelle ignored Wrench to skip to Jenny. "You're all wet!" she exclaimed, as if she wasn't equally soaked.

"Say," Laura said suddenly. "How'd you do that?"

Jenny realized Laura was talking to her. "Do what?"

"Shift your dress with you. You were dressed when you got free from that jerk with the wings."

Jenny looked down at herself. The sundress and her sandals had indeed shifted with her, without any conscious thought. "I don't know," she said in surprise.

"I'm a very good teacher," Gizelle said proudly.

"Can you clothing shift, too?" Laura asked her. "I thought it was only dragons and mythical creatures that could do that."

Gizelle blinked, then shook her head. "Nope," she said airily.

"Then how did you... never mind." Laura shook her head firmly. "Tex, I'd like a hot drink with a gallon of alcohol now, please."

Tex tipped his sodden hat to her. "Yes'm!"

Gizelle trailed after them to the bar. "Can I have some?" she asked innocently.

"I'll make you a hot chocolate, fawn," Tex told her. "Wrench, can I get you something?"

That left Jenny standing along with Travis, and she was glad when he slipped his hand into hers. The clouds above them had thinned, and though it was still raining lightly, the wind had died down and shafts of sunlight turned the wet leaves and gleaming tiles to jewels and treasure. Jenny suspected that if she looked around, she'd find a rainbow somewhere, but she didn't want to look anywhere but the smiling face of her mate.

"Hungry?" he suggested.

"Yes," she answered with a playful smile.

Oh, yes, agreed her otter.

He smiled back down at her. "Hot shower first?"

"Mm, yes," Jenny agreed, picturing his naked body in a

cascade of hot water and foamy soap. "And then something out of the staff fridge would be plenty. Maybe Breck
still has some cake stashed in there."

Travis bent down and kissed her. "I can think of something that tastes sweeter…"

EPILOGUE

$\mathscr{T}$ravis put down his tools and stepped back to get perspective on their progress.

The last ravages of the storm had been all but erased from the resort. Graham had carefully pruned back the most obvious breakage and groomed the lawns, with help from Gizelle. An impressive pile of dead brush and branches had been stashed near the beach to dry for their next bonfire.

There were a few broken windows that were waiting for replacements from the mainland, but Travis and Wrench had repaired most of the roofs, mopped up the water damage, and started to fix the facade damage done to the spa. The man had proven himself quick to pick up on the things Travis taught him, as well as a hard worker. He seemed determined to make up for kidnapping Jenny, and Travis was inclined to forgive him. He'd coaxed enough parts of the man's story from him to be sympathetic, though he still didn't know who he would have been buying dance lessons for, or how he'd ended up in jail the first time; prying personal information out of him would require something stronger than an impact driver.

"Let's stop here and take lunch," he suggested, keenly aware of a certain item in his pocket and the hole it was burning there. "We're getting to the hottest point of the day and there's still a few days worth of work here."

Wrench scowled. "I'm okay to work longer."

"Are you trying to make me look bad?" Travis laughed. "Seriously, the job will wait."

"Yeah, okay." Wrench looked past Travis and nodded understanding at the same time Travis recognized Jenny's presence behind him.

"I was just taking a break from my work and thought I'd come see if you wanted to take a picnic lunch in the gardens," Jenny suggested when he turned to grin foolishly at her. She was a vision in a simple silk wrap that made every curve look perfect. She had a basket over one forearm.

He suspected the picnic lunch she had packed was the second course to the meal she had in mind; merriment danced in her eyes.

"I'll pack up the tools," Wrench offered gruffly.

"How's the work going?" Jenny asked, twining her fingers with Travis' as they walked away. He remembered how embarrassed she'd been when she hadn't been able to shift the webbing between her fingers. She was so amazing, so capable, so in control now.

"We're waiting on some things from the mainland — it takes longer now that we don't have our own boat — but the rest is nearly all done. Just some cosmetic stuff at the spa to finish up. How's your work going?"

"It's quite a puzzle," Jenny told him enthusiastically. "I've never seen a contract with some of these specific terms, and there are references to some older documents.

I'm having the firm run a search for the ones that may be relevant. At a glance, there are some weird loopholes that *would* allow Beehag's lawyer to legally take the resort lease out from under Scarlet, but the requirements are crazy specific. It's going to take some more research to be sure about any of it."

She was alive with excitement about the topic, eyes sparkling and her feet skipping eagerly over the gravel as they walked. Seeing her so happy made him feel a hundred feet tall and on top of the world.

It also made him want to kiss her, and slip the dress strap off her shoulder, so he was happy when they arrived at the garden and Jenny put the picnic lunch down on the bench and stood on tiptoe to slip her arms around his neck.

When Travis had finished claiming her mouth for his own, he suggested reluctantly, "Lunch first?"

"I'm having my first course now," Jenny answered. "The rest will keep."

He was hard against her, desperately hungry for the meal she offered, but he still drew back when she would have kissed him again, pulling his shirt from his pants.

"Wait," he said.

She paused, searching his eyes. "What's wrong?"

"Nothing in the world," Travis assured her. "Everything is perfect. Which is why I want to do this…"

He reached into the cargo pocket of his pants; it was a small box he'd been carrying around all day, since it had come express mail with the last charter plane.

Jenny looked at it curiously, then raised surprised and suspicious dark eyes to his.

Travis cleared his throat. "I love you, Jenny," he said without preamble. "I know you'll need to return to LA to give testimony in the next few months and I thought you might want to go up to Alaska afterwards and meet my family."

"Meet your family?" Jenny repeated, a slow, cautious smile blooming on her beautiful face.

"As my bride," Travis added. He popped the box open to display the modest diamond ring.

Jenny gave a wordless squeak, clasping her hands over her mouth.

"Crap," Travis remembered, hastily dropping to one knee. "I was going to kneel for that part."

He pulled the ring from its velvet casing, thinking too hard about other velvet casings, and offered it to Jenny.

Jenny gave him a trembling hand, nodding wordlessly, and Travis slipped the ring onto her finger.

"It fits perfectly," she breathed, smiling with her whole face.

"It's useful being able to quiz your twin sister for information," Travis confessed, as he stood.

Jenny grinned. "Oh, how'd Tex take that pressure?"

"Cussed me out for beating him to the punch like I didn't even know that cowboy was capable of."

"Did he mention the possibility of a double wedding?" Jenny asked.

Sensing a trap, Travis searched her eyes. "Do you want one?" he asked cautiously.

Jenny looked seriously back. "As a teenager who was sick of being a twin, I would have wanted to kill you for suggesting it. But now?" her face softened. "I sort of like the idea. I wouldn't have met you if I hadn't come to save Laura and Tex. And they wouldn't have met if Laura hadn't been pretending to be me. If Laura and Tex wanted to, I'd do it."

"We could have the ceremony in the gardens, a reception on the bar deck, if you wanted," Travis suggested.

"Ceremony on the beach," Jenny counter-offered. "I want this garden to be our place, alone."

Travis bent down to kiss her. "I'd be fine getting married by the dumpsters behind the kitchen," he said easily.

Jenny scrunched her face at him. "I would not be okay with that."

"So picky," Travis grouched merrily.

Jenny put her arms around his neck and kissed him soundly. He could not get enough of the taste and feel of her that close. He pressed his hard cock against her, drinking up the lush curves of her through her thin dress.

When she drew back after a moment, Travis felt it as keenly as if he'd lost something.

But she didn't go far, gazing into his eyes. "I love you, Travis," she said seriously. "I am so happy to be marrying you."

"I love you, Jennavivianna Rose," he told her just as seriously back. He had loved her full name from the first moment he'd heard it.

Her face lit up with mischief. "Want to crush a flowerbed?"

Travis gathered her back into his arms in answer, sweeping her off of her feet and back into the nearest bank of flowers, peeling her dress over her head as he lay her down.

She pulled his shirt off over his head and tugged at the waistband of his pants. "Why are you still wearing these?" she teased.

Travis was happy to facilitate their removal, and then his free member, thick and firm, was pressing at his lover's entrance, letting the anticipation build.

Jenny squirmed beneath him, and the flowers crushed beneath her were fragrant and green and Travis knew that he would never be able to smell this scent or walk through this garden without thinking of his gorgeous mate and the way that he loved her and wanted to protect her forever.

"Travis," she whined beneath him, arching and trying to take him into her.

"Jennavivian—" He didn't finish before she had succeeded in raising herself around him, and his world narrowed to the feeling of being in her, of joining with her as intimately as it was possibly for two souls to be.

"I love you," Jenny said near his ear, breathless and needy.

Travis fell into her completely.

~

*T*hank you for reading my book! Continue the story in Tropical Dragon Diver, or read on for a sneak preview! If you'd like bonus epilogue scenes from several of my books, be sure to join my mailing list.

A NOTE FROM ZOE CHANT

I hope you enjoyed Travis and Jenny's book! Thank you so much for reading it!

I always love to know what you thought — you can leave a review at Amazon (I read every one, and they help other readers find me, too!) or email me at zoechantebooks@ gmail.com.

If you'd like to be emailed when I release my next book, please click here to be added to my mailing list. You can also visit my webpage, or follow me on Facebook. You are also invited to join my VIP Readers Group on Facebook, where I show off new covers first, and you can get sneak previews and ask questions.

Keep reading for a preview chapter from the next book in the Shifting Sands Resort series, *Tropical Dragon Diver*, where Bastian will find his dearest treasure!

The cover of *Tropical Lynx's Lover* was designed by Ellen Million (visit her page to find coloring pages of some of my characters, including Gizelle and Graham!).

WRITING AS ELVA BIRCH

A Day Care for Shifters: A hot new full-length series about adorable shifter kids and their struggling single parents in a town full of mystery and surprise. Start the series with Wolf's Instinct, when Addison comes to Nickel City to take a job at a very special day care and finds a family to belong to. Funny and full of feeling, this is a gentle ice-cream-straight-from-the-container escape. Sweet and sizzling!

The Royal Dragons of Alaska: A fascinating alternate world where Alaska is ruled by secret dragon shifters. Adventure, romance, and humor! Reluctant royalty, relentless enemies… dogs, camping, and magic! Start with The Dragon Prince of Alaska.

Suddenly Shifters: A hilarious series of novellas, serials, and shorts set in the small town of Anders Canyon, where something (in the water?) is making ordinary citizens turn into shifters. Start with Something in the Water! Also available in audio!

Lawn Ornament Shifters: The series that was only supposed to be a joke, this is a collection of short, ridiculous romances featuring unusual shifters, myths, and magic. Cross-your-legs funny and full of heart! Start with The Flamingo's Fated Mate!

~

Birch Hearts: An enchanting collection of short stories and novellas. Unconstrained by theme or setting, each short read has romance, magic, and heart, with a satisfying conclusion. And always, the impossible and irresistible. Start with a sampler plate in Prompted 2 for fourteen pieces of sweet-to-sizzling flash fiction, or the novella, Better Half. Breakup is a free story!

MORE BY ZOE CHANT

Shifting Sands Resort: A complete ten-book series - plus two collections of shorts. This is a sizzling shifter romance set at a tropical island resort. Each book stands alone but connects into a great mystery with a thrilling conclusion. Start with Tropical Tiger Spy or dive in to the Omnibus edition, with all of the novels, short stories, and novellas in my preferred reading order! Shifting Sands Resort crosses over with Fire and Rescue Shifters and Shifter Kingdom.

Fae Shifter Knights: A complete four-book fantasy portal romp, with cute pets and swoon-worthy knights stuck in a world of wonders like refrigerators and ham sandwiches. Start with Dragon of Glass!

Green Valley Shifters: A sweet, small town series with single dads, secret shifters, sweet kids, and spinsters. Low-peril and steamy! Standalone books where you can revisit your favorite characters - this series is also complete with six books! Start with Dancing Bearfoot! This series crosses over with **Virtue Shifters**, which starts with Timber Wolf.

SUPPORT ME ON PATREON

What is Patreon?

Patreon is a site where readers and fans can support creators with monthly subscriptions.

At my Patreon, I have tiers with early rough drafts of my books, flash fiction, coloring pages, signed and sketched paperbacks, exclusive swag, original artwork, photographs…and so much more! Every month is a little different, and there is a price for every budget. Patreon allows me to do projects that aren't very commercial and makes my income stream a little less unpredictable. It also gives me a place to connect with my fans!

Come find out what's going on behind the scenes and keep me creating at Patreon! patreon.com/ellenmillion

SNEAK PREVIEW OF THE
DRAGON PRINCE OF ALASKA...

Writing as Elva Birch.

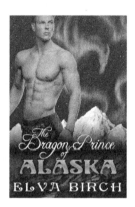

Carina Andresen surged to her feet, sweeping her camp
chair out from under her as a make-shift weapon.

Wolf! her brain hammered at her. *Wolf!* She was going
to become an Alaska tourist statistic and get eaten by a
wolf on her second week in the kingdom.

Logic slowly caught up with her panic.

The animal across the campfire from her was smaller
and *doggier* than a wolf, and it was only a moment before
Carina could get her breath and heartbeat back under
control and recognize that it was well-groomed, shyly
eyeing her sizzling hot dog, and wagging its tail.

Alaska probably had stray dogs, too; she wasn't *that* far
from civilization.

"Hi there, sweetie," Carina said, her voice still unnaturally high as she put her chair back on its legs. "Does that smell good? Want a bit of hot dog?" Carina turned the hot dog in the flame and waggled it suggestively.

The non-edible dog sped up his tail and when Carina broke off a piece of the meat and dropped it beside her, he crept around the fire and slurped it eagerly up off the ground.

The second bite he took gently from her fingers, and by the second hot dog she dared to pet him.

Within about thirty minutes and five hot dogs, he was leaning on her and letting her scratch his ears and neck as he wagged his tail and groaned in delight.

"Oh, you're just a dear," Carina said. "I bet someone's missing you." He was a husky mix, Carina guessed; he was tall and strong, with a long, thick coat of dark gray fur and white feet. His ears were upright, and his tail was long and feathered. He didn't have a collar, but he was clearly friendly. "You want some water?"

The dog licked his lips as if he had understood, and Carina carefully stood so she didn't frighten him.

But he seemed to be past any shyness now, and he followed Carina to her van trustingly, tail waving happily. He drank the offered water from a frying pan, and then tried to give Carina a kiss dripping with slobber.

"You probably already have a name," Carina said, laughingly trying to escape the wet tongue. "But I'm going to call you Shadow for now." She had a grubby towel hanging from her clothesline and used it to dry off his face. They played a gentle game of tug-of-war, testing each other's strength and manners.

Shadow seemed to approve of his new name and gave her a canine grin once she'd won the towel back from him.

"Alright, Shadow, let's go collect some more firewood."

The area was rich with downed wood to harvest, and with the assistance of a folding hand saw, Carina was able to find several heaping armloads of solid, dry wood, enough to keep a cheerful fire going for a few days if she was frugal. It was comforting to have Shadow around for the task; she wasn't quite as nervous about the noises she heard, and he was a happy distraction from her own brain.

He frolicked with her, and found a stick three times his own length to drag around possessively.

"So helpful!" Carina laughed at him, as he knocked over an empty pot and swiped her across the knees so that she nearly fell.

When she sat down beside the crackling fire in her low camp chair, Shadow abandoned his prize stick and crowded close to lay his head on her knee. Carina petted him absently.

"Someone's looking for you, you big softy," she said regretfully. She would have to try to reunite the dog with his owner but, for now, it was nice having a companion around the camp.

Of all the things she expected when she went running for the wilderness, she had never guessed that the silence would be the worst. She had been camping plenty, but it was always *with* someone. Since their parents had died, that someone was usually her sister, June, but sometimes it was a friend or a roommate. She was used to having someone to point out birds and animals to, someone to share chores with, stretch out tarps with. When it was just her, the spaces seemed vaster, the wind bit harder, and even the birds were less cheerful.

"You probably don't care about the birds that would make my life list," she told Shadow mournfully.

Shadow wagged his tail in a rustle of leaves.

She didn't have her life list anymore to add to anyway.

Everything had been left behind: her phone, her computer, her identity. Her entire life was on hold. She had the van to live in, some supplies and a small nest egg to start from, so she ought to be able to stay out of sight long enough to regroup and...she didn't know what to do from here. Find a journalist willing to take her story and clear her name?

To fill the quiet, and to help ignore the ache in her chest, she read aloud from the brochure on Alaska that she had been given at the border station. She'd found it that evening while she was emptying the glovebox to take stock of supplies, and Shadow seemed as good a listener as any.

"Like many modern monarchies, Alaska has an elected council of officials who do most of the day to day rulings of this vast, rich land. The royal family is steeped in tradition and mystery, and holds many veto powers, as well as acting as ambassadors to other countries. Known as the Dragon King, the Alaskan sovereign is a reserved figure who rarely appears in public. Margaret, the Queen of Alaska, died twelve years ago, leaving behind six sons." There was a photo, with boys ranging from about seven to maybe twenty-five. Two of the middle children were identical. One of the twins was wearing a hockey jersey and grinning, the other wore glasses and looked annoyed. The oldest—or at least the tallest—was frowning seriously at the others. The only blonde of the bunch was one of the middle boys, who was looking intently at the camera. The youngest looked painfully bored. They all had tongue-twisting names of more syllables than Carina wanted to try pronouncing.

Carina thought it was an interesting photo. The tension between the oldest two was palpable, and the they were all dressed surprisingly casually. She didn't follow royal gossip much beyond scanning headlines at grocery store checkouts, but Alaska never seemed to make waves; they were rarely involved in dramas and scandals.

Shadow raised his head and cocked his head at some imagined noise in the forest.

"That's a lot of siblings," Carina observed, ruffling his ears. She felt so much safer having him beside her. "Just one sister was more than enough for me." She didn't want to admit how much she missed that sister right now.

Shadow returned his head to her knee. "Alaska is a member of the Small Kingdoms Alliance, an exclusive collective of independent monarchies scattered throughout the world. Although Alaska has large amounts of land, they qualify for membership because of their small population."

Carina turned the brochure over. "There are hot springs about fifty miles north of Fairbanks! I hope to make it there." *Before* she ran out of cash. It looked expensive. Maybe she could get work there...she'd heard that it wasn't hard to find under-the-table jobs in this country.

Shadow suddenly leapt to his feet, barking at something crashing through the woods behind them and Carina nearly tipped over backwards in her camp chair trying to stand up.

She expected to find a moose, or possibly a bear, and she was already picking up the chair to use as a flimsy defense against a charging wild animal.

But it was only a man stepping out of the woods, in an official dark blue uniform emblazoned with the eight gold stars of Alaska.

For a moment, terror every bit as keen as the panic that had gripped her at the first sight of Shadow washed over her. They'd found her.

"You're trespassing on royal land and I'm going to have to ask you to leave," he said.

Then she realized with relief that it wasn't a police officer. He was only a park ranger.

~

...or was he? Discover love and adventure in a wonderful alternate Alaska with camping and dogs and magic, reluctant royalty and relentless enemies! Pick up The Dragon Prince of Alaska *today!*

SNEAK PREVIEW: TROPICAL DRAGON DIVER

BY ZOE CHANT

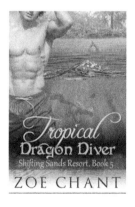

The last notes of her song were fading out of the room as Saina rose carefully from the foot of the bed.

The man at the other end of the bed remained still, one arm flung back on his pillow as he drooled on it. Saina nudged him with a finger and decided with relief he would probably sleep for a while. Her lullaby had done its work, and he'd fallen asleep without laying one greasy finger on her.

If she was lucky, he'd be snoring for a few hours, and

wake up not the slightest bit wiser for his little nap, every memory of Saina and her music nothing more than a distant fantasy. She gathered the skimpy dressing gown around her shoulders and drew in a breath.

It was a big room, for a boat, but it wasn't big enough to hide much in. The safe in the closet gave her a moment of pause, but she knew that what she was really after wouldn't fit in the shoebox-sized compartment, so she continued her hunt until she found the suitcase under the bunk. It was locked, but too ridiculously heavy for its size to be clothing. The handcuff hanging open off the handle made Saina certain this was her goal.

She slipped her hairpin kit out of her dark, upswept hair and wriggled it into the lock, grateful that it wasn't a digital system. A few careful movements, listening diligently, and the tumblers fell away and clicked open. Saina unsnapped the clasps and tipped the lid back to expose bricks of pale gray, plastic-wrapped, just as it had been described.

This was it.

She sat back on her heels. She hated this whole job, every part of it was distasteful and wrong, even if the people on this yacht were all low-life smugglers who deserved no better. But her directions had been very specific and her Voice… her Voice needed her. No one else was going to come to her rescue, so it was up to Saina.

She went to the closet and got the lurid pink carry-on she had bought the week before, emptying its contents on the floor.

The bricks all but filled it, leaving room for one dress smashed on top, and her evening purse with her phone and makeup. The rest of the clothing, she stuffed into the handcuffed suitcase, shoving what was left to the very back of the closet.

Saina paused at the doorway and cracked the door, and was glad to see that the short hallway was empty. Sounds of carousing still came from the lounge towards the bow of the yacht, and she crept down the stairs towards the stern, pulling the luggage behind her as quietly as she could manage.

Two guards were standing outside the door out onto the back deck, smoking cigarettes and talking loudly.

Saina observed them through the windows, and looked past them to the dinghy tied along the side of the boat. It was pitch black out, in the very early hours of the morning. The tropical air was warm and thick with humidity. She suspected that a storm was coming.

Saina chewed on her cheek for a moment, considering her options. There weren't many. She sighed, sucked her breath in, loosened her dressing gown, and sauntered out of the door like she owned it.

Her appearance arrested their conversation, and she heaved a dramatic sigh, nearly upsetting her breasts out of the skimpy lingerie she was wearing. "Good evening, boys," she singsonged.

"It's that lounge singer Anders picked up at Jaco yesterday," one of them recognized.

"And what a bore that guy was," Saina said, giving them both appraising looks. Anders hadn't gotten anything more from her than a nap, but they wouldn't know that. She put one hand on her round hip and inspected her fingernails on the other.

They stared, cigarettes hanging at the edges of their mouths, before exchanging looks. Saina immediately dubbed them Skeptical and Hopeful in her head, based on their expressions.

Skeptical eyed her overloaded rolling luggage curiously, while Hopeful couldn't stop staring at the cleavage spilling out of the frilly little number she was wearing. Saina turned her attention on Skeptical, humming lightly under her breath.

"You looking to give us a little private show?" Hopeful suggested gleefully.

Saina answered with a few bars of an appropriate pop song:

"Are you looking
    For a good time?
    Have you got yourself
    A thin dime?"

By the time she hit the second chorus, they were both swaying in place, the smile on Skeptical's face as broad and entranced as Hopeful's.

She kept singing as she went to work, persuading them with her song that nothing out of the ordinary was happening. There was nothing to see, they were simply lost in a simple fantasy of their own imagination. It would have been easier to simply drown them than to keep singing, like any one of her sisters would have, but Saina couldn't bring herself to do that.

Not even to drug-running scumbag mercenaries like this.

She pulled the pink bag behind her to the stern of the ship and lifted the cowling off the inboard motor. It took only a few strong yanks to disconnect the fuel and easy-to-reach electronics, and Saina used a fire extinguisher to dent the ignition mechanism so it wouldn't be an easy fix. The last thing she wanted was for them to be able to follow her. A glance showed that the disruptions to her song as she worked hadn't broken the spell over Skeptical and

Hopeful, but she knew she didn't have much time or breath left.

Hauling the dinghy down from its rack and getting it over the side of the boat was a Herculean task, and Saina wished, not for the first time, that sensible shoes fit with the image she was trying to attain.

The dinghy splashed into the water, and Saina struggled to get the heavy luggage over after it, her song stuttering with the effort.

Then, as she drew in a breath to get Skeptical and Hopeful back on track, her luck ran out.

On the deck above, there was a sudden shout and Saina looked up in alarm to spot another guard, this one with a girl hanging on his arm, dressed much as she was and looking vacant and tipsy.

Saina weighed her options. She wasn't sure that she could enspell the guard before others came to his alarm cry, and she wasn't sure how many more she would be able to sing insensible — she'd already spent more of her energy than she anticipated. Instead of standing her ground, she kicked off her heels and vaulted over the edge of the boat into the wobbly dinghy. She flipped out the choke and yanked the tiny outboard to life.

The guard's shouts intensified, and Saina heard others answer. Hopeful and Skeptical shook off the last of her song in confusion. Frantically, she pointed the dinghy away from the yacht and kicked it up to high gear, cursing its powerless motor and slow speed.

Still, the yacht and the shouting began to drop away in the darkness behind her, and Saina breathed a sigh of relief. Maybe she would actually get away with this. Maybe...

Distant shots fired and bullets shattered the air around

her. Saina dived to the bottom of the inflatable boat, covering her head and biting her lip against her cries of fear as they blasted around her for a length of time that seemed impossibly long. They couldn't see her in the darkness, so the shots were wild, and she knew that was her only saving grace. As it was, the boat lurched sickeningly and she knew it had been hit. She could only hope that it had multiple flotation pockets, and that what hadn't been compromised was enough to keep her afloat until she could get somewhere safe.

The motor hummed blissfully on, pushing her further and further away from the disabled yacht, and the shots became more and sporadic as the shouts got more distant. Saina's cries of fear turned to sobs of pathetic relief as she thought she might escape with her life.

She crouched again, leaning to one side as the boat, clearly deflating on the other side, tipped and sagged. She scanned the water ahead, hopeful for lights, but saw nothing.

Behind her, another few shots rang out, and she was driven forward, nearly out of the boat, as pain and fire bloomed to one side of her back.

Bastian drew in a deep breath of salty air. It was already windy, and he could smell the storm that was coming, though the sky above was still clear and sunny.

A sensible dragon would be taking cover, going to ground while the winds were too high to fly in. It was the sort of day to curl in one's hoard and count precious things, while the weather became wet and unfriendly.

But Bastian was no kind of sensible dragon.

In human form, he passed the empty pool deck, double-checking that the lounge chairs had all been secured and the towel cabinets were shut and latched. The bottles of sunscreen and lotion had all been stashed away, and the kickboards and pool floats were all behind doors. The sign declaring no lifeguard was on duty was already up, flapping noisily in the rising wind. Bastian grinned at it. A storm, rare here, meant a day off, and he was going to make the most of it.

He walked along the strangely bare deck. The few guests, like dragons, would be tucked away in their safe cottages, avoiding the wind and weather. As for the other staff, Bastian had no idea where they were, but he was just as glad not to encounter them and have to explain where he was going.

The steps down to the beach were littered with loose sand and Bastian shifted as he walked down them. One step was a sandaled foot, the next, a claw that spanned three of the white concrete steps. He may not be the largest dragon from his family, but he was far from the smallest. His scales gleamed green and gold, faceted like jewels.

Bastian paused at the lifeguard tower, taking a moment to appreciate the familiar view. The beach swept to either side, white sand stretching to meet sapphire water. The little beach bar was shuttered up, all the chairs safely inside. The dock was empty; the resort owner, Scarlet, had not replaced the boat that had been destroyed the week before.

He swiveled his head to look behind him. He was tall enough in dragon form to look easily onto the tiled pool deck, a useful trait as a lifeguard that enabled him to watch both swimming areas. Above the pool deck, the vacant bar deck looked down, and above that the restaurant deck. The steep structure of the Costa Rican island meant the resort was built in tiers, and it gleamed white in the sun.

The palm trees framing the pool were beginning to whip in the building wind, and Bastian could see the dark clouds beginning to gather behind the crest of the hill above him.

A dragon face wasn't arranged for grinning, but Bastian's inner human certainly was.

He had the day for himself.

He had the wide ocean for himself.

He walked down by the dock, where the ocean fell away more quickly than the swimming and sunbathing area and he could wade in and begin swimming almost at once.

At first, the swimming was awkward, clawed feet and powerful legs were not arranged for paddling, and wings, even tucked tightly against his side, dragged on the waves and wind.

Then Bastian sucked in a deep breath and dived, pulling all his limbs against his body and letting his massive tail propel him fully under.

No longer divided between air and ocean, he cut through the water as if he'd been born there, not a creature of fire, but of saltwater.

He had to surface near the breakwater; it grew too shallow there to stay beneath the waves, and he climbed over the rocks and paused, shaking water droplets off his big head and spreading his massive wings before he tucked them against his body again and returned to the element he preferred.

Fish scattered before him, and a pod of dolphins gave him wide berth, but Bastian paid them no mind. His human had eaten well from the resort kitchen and he had no need for legless prey this fine morning.

He was on a different kind of hunt, instead, and as he drifted along the sandy ocean floor, still holding his breath, he closed his eyes and let other senses take over.

At first, there was nothing, then, like distant musical notes, he felt the first tingle of treasure.

His lungs cried out for air, and Bastian oriented himself and returned to the surface to refill. However he loved the water, he still required air, like any dragon.

He dived down in the direction of the pull once he had sucked in a big breath.

The bit of treasure gave itself easily up to his big claws, digging down through the deep sand, and Bastian did a lightning fast shift so he could tuck it into his human form's belt pouch and shift back before he opened his senses to the next one.

Each time he returned to the surface for air, the waves and wind were rougher and rougher, once even breaking directly into his face as he was sucking in his breath.

He coughed and sputtered, thinking wryly that his family would feel vindicated if he died by drowning. That alone made him stubbornly decide to stay out in the storm. He floated at the surface, bobbing on the giant swells as he refilled his lungs and prepared to dive again.

A sudden wave of treasure sense broke over him more strongly than the wave of saltwater had. It dwarfed the little tingles that had called him earlier, and Bastian almost swamped himself responding to it.

There was a shark, he realized, as he dove back into the water, then he was surprised to sense another through the waves, until he realized that beneath the treasure sense was something else: blood.

He was not quite as fast as a shark, but Bastian put every ounce of his swimming strength into cutting the distance between his goal and himself.

By the time he got there, swimming up from beneath,

there were three sharks circling what Bastian realized was a half-deflated dinghy, adrift without power and reeking of treasure and the iron tang of blood.

He could not roar underwater, nor flame the sharks, but he could growl, and the water took the vibrations of his claim to the interlopers.

The sharks circled one last time in confusion, then retreated some distance, continuing to swirl just out of his reach.

Bastian had no interest in them, and considered them no threat. Even without flame, he was a dragon, many times their size and strength, and no stranger to the ocean. He had claws like swords, and his jewel-faceted scales were solid protection against their teeth.

He surfaced to inspect his spoils, refilling his lungs.

The sad, wilted dinghy had clearly taken a beating, and it was being tossed on the wild waves, making it difficult to get close. Bastian's treasure sense was threatening to overwhelm him. There was something precious and rare here.

When a wave washed over the dinghy, sloshing into the bed of the boat and what lay there, instinct made Bastian open his mouth and challenge the ocean itself with a roar. This was his, his treasure, his to crown his hoard with.

The uncaring ocean answered by slapping another wave at him, driving the half-limp boat up against his chest.

Finally, Bastian could look into the boat itself, and he dismissed the lurid pink suitcase that was deforming the bottom of the boat without a second thought; his treasure was not in the heavy luggage. It was the figure, a limp woman wearing something flimsy and soaking wet, plastered to every lush curve. Her long dark hair was loose around her shoulders like a cloak. She was face-down in the boat, barely breathing, and even in the storm-dark,

Bastian could see that blood had dyed the water in the boat dark crimson.

He carefully rolled her over, using a dragon claw like a surgical tool, and her face was the most beautiful golden color that he had ever seen.

This is our mate, he realized in wonder.

His human added anxiously, *She's been shot*!

Bastian could see that she had a wound, still oozing sharp-smelling blood, just above her heart. His human was alarmed at the amount of the blood she must have lost so far, but Bastian only knew that she was every treasure he had ever sought, and that he must take her safely to his hoard and give her everything that he had.

Another wave threatened to rip the sinking boat away from him, just as the clouds above opened up and began to drench them in rain.

Bastian snatched the woman up into his forearms as the tortured boat began to sink, and his human helpfully suggested how to keep her above the water without jostling her injury further.

We don't know if that bullet is still in her, his human warned him, but Bastian didn't need a reminder to treat her gently.

He couldn't fly with her, not through weather like this, so he continued on his back, using his tail to propel them. Here, along the surface, travel was agonizing slow, and waves broke over them several times, washing away the blood as they traveled. Bastian felt like he could hear a song at intervals, low beneath the roar of the storm.

It was hours of this unpleasant travel, feeling the weak beat of her heart against the scales of his chest, before Shifting Sands came into view once more. Bastian lifted her into one forearm as his back legs found purchase under him. The wavebreak was as tall as he was, but he wrapped his wings forward around her protectively and carried her carefully to shore.

The wind was finally beginning to die down as he got her up to the shelter of the bar. Tex was there, taking stock of the storm damage. If he was surprised to see Bastian away from the beach in dragon form, that was nothing to the surprise on his face when Bastian slowly lowered his prize onto the floor, bleeding and wet...

Read the rest of Tropical Dragon Diver now!

Made in the USA
Coppell, TX
15 April 2024